MURDER
at the
TOKYO
LAWN TENNIS CLUB

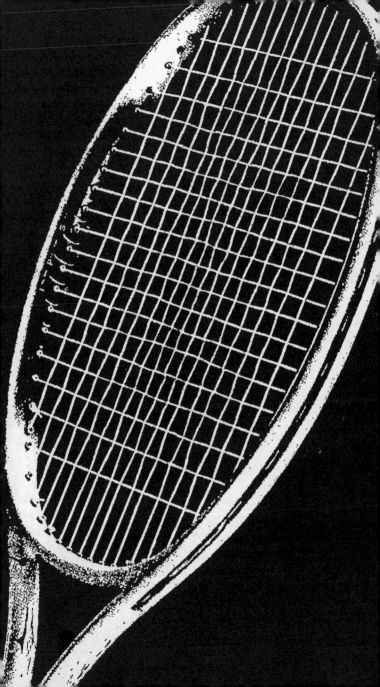

MURDER

at the
TOKYO
LAWN TENNIS CLUB

ROBERT J. COLLINS

YENBOOKS

YENBOOKS are published and distributed by
the Charles E. Tuttle Company, Inc. with
editorial offices at 2-6 Suido 1-chome,
Bunkyo-ku, Tokyo 112, Japan

First YENBOOKS edition, 1994

LCC Card No. 93-61584
ISBN 0-8048-1934-3

Printed in Japan

To Keiko
a lobber if there ever was one

Shig Manabe was one of the nicest guys in the world. You would have to search far and wide to find anybody with a bad thing to say about the man. Some people, for no earthly reason, are like that.

All this is not to say that Shig had been living the life of a recluse. He had been involved in some of the more momentous events of his day and age.

Born in Yokohama, Shig moved with his family to Seattle as a ten-year-old. His father was employed by a Japanese trading company, and Shig quickly adapted to the American way of life. As a grade-school and junior high student in the relatively somnolent years before World War II, he fancied baggy trousers, wore brown-and-white saddle shoes, and cheered for the old Seattle Rainiers of the Pacific Coast Baseball League.

The Manabe family beat a hasty retreat back to Japan in early 1942, but the *sayonara* party for Shig at his school was not without a few tears from his teenage classmates. He was even awarded his varsity letter in baseball weeks before the annual sports banquet.

Finishing high school in Japan had not been easy. English was completely banned, and Shig's Japanese language skills were rusty at best. But he kept his head down, went through all the correct motions, and avoided having the daylights beat out of him by those sensitive to the subtleties and nuances of "foreign pollution."

Shig graduated from high school in 1944 and was immediately drafted into the Imperial Army. Not being particularly keen to shoot people, Shig volunteered for an elite corps of personnel deployed as translators and interrogators. (Careful not to reveal too much under the circumstances, Shig demonstrated his English skills with the sentence: "Shoot the Babe Ruth bastards from the sky down and kill.") He got the assignment and sat patiently as he underwent intensive language training from men who had learned English from a book.

The tour of duty in China was not without its difficulties. The most trying aspect was interrogating a group of prisoners that included his old physical education instructor from Seattle. Shig shared his ration of rice, soup, and bamboo shoots with the man. (As history was later to record, Shig was eventually given the key to the city by the mayor of Seattle.)

Shig became a prisoner of war in September 1945 and was returned to Japan in time to experience one of the most severe winters in Tokyo history. After various interviews with the Occupation forces, Shig was released from prison and hired to translate documents and official pronouncements. At the time he weighed 45 kilograms—down from his high school weight of 70 kilograms.

People seemed to like Shig, and eventually trusted him. His scholarship to the University of Michigan was the direct result of friendships developed during the Occupation. He received his bachelor's degree and married a classmate—the daughter of a pearl importer from New York—on the same day. Shig wore a yarmulke at the wedding, along with his formal kimono. The newlyweds settled in Manhattan's Upper West Side.

Shig got involved. Down through the years he was an active member of the American Heart Association and served on the board of the New York Home for Foundling Children for ten years. He even raised money for the Republican Party in New York State.

The pearl business had been good to Shig and now, at sixty-eight and semiretired, he divided his time between Tokyo and New York. When in Tokyo, his favorite haunt was the Tokyo Lawn Tennis Club. If anything, he probably had more friends there than anywhere.

The tennis game that day had not been altogether satisfying. Shig and his regular partner, known collectively as the Silver Foxes, had built up a 5–3 lead in the first set, but they blew it and lost 5–7. The Silver Foxes really came apart in the second set and lost 1–6. A basic fact of life is that the strategy and skills of veterans are often obliterated by the speed and strength of youth.

A hot Japanese bath after a day of exercise is one of life's great sensual pleasures. The temperature in the *ofuro* was just right. Shig's head leaned against the rim of the tub—his body stretched out—with his toes emerging from the water at the other end. Those toes had been through a lot—shuffling back and forth to school in wooden sandals, running around bases in ill-fitting baseball shoes, tromping in rotting dampness through jungles, standing in cardboard on icy pavement, and chasing diabolical drop shots in tennis. The second toe on the right foot was a particular problem, having been shattered by a bullet through the boot during the surrender ceremonies in China.

Locker room sounds—the banging of doors and the rumblings of athletes excusing performance—filled the air. The pervasive smell of liniment was everywhere.

Unfortunately, none of these thoughts and sensations registered with Shig Manabe. One of the all-time good guys, about whom nary an evil word was spoken, was up to his eyebrows in the bath—now turning pink and beginning to bubble crimson. The American Heart Association, the New York Home for Foundling Children, even the Republican Party in New York State were on their own. No locks in Seattle would ever again be opened by Shig's keys.

On the floor next to the bath was Shig's tennis racket, a dynamically balanced graphite model with impedance tension and a shock-absorbing grip (designed to reduce the incidence of tennis elbow). The rim of the racket, it was later determined, bore traces of decidedly nontennis activity—blood, matted hair, and microscopic chunks of brain matter from the skull of the one of the nicest guys in the world.

CHAPTER 2

The fact that Shig's body was initially discovered by Nat Forrest, a junior member of the club and occasional partner of Shig's, delayed rational response to the tragedy for several minutes. Nothing would have changed the fact of Shig's death, of course, but the considerable turmoil introduced by Nat's immediate reaction to the situation would have been avoided.

Nat, not wearing his glasses, went as far as stepping into the bath with one foot before comprehending the circumstances as presented. His subsequent hysterical explosion from the bath area, the accompanying screams and gestures, and the long slide on the locker room floor ending with a head-banging crash against the building's main support beam created something of a diversion amongst the locker room denizens. In fact, the honorable Tatsuo Morimoto, club president, was still waving a towel over the semiconscious Nat Forrest five minutes later when a decision was made to call an ambulance—for Nat.

A few more minutes were spent by the locker room denizens discussing the peculiar behavior of foreigners and their unexpected outbursts. The club was composed of about fifty percent foreigners, but the Japanese members still found themselves wrestling almost daily with bicultural anomalies and mysteries. In all fairness, the Japanese members were an internationalized crowd—many had lived abroad and most had traveled abroad—nevertheless, there were still surprising and unpredictable behavioral developments.

In this case, an American was on the floor, clearly crazed, naked as the day he was born, and babbling about his foot, a headache, and "bodies underwater." What, when it comes right down to it, could be more difficult?

Matters didn't come to a head until a fourth-generation Japanese resident named Kim—still a Korean and make no mistake about that—wandered into the bath and rediscovered Shig.

The locker room denizens rushed to the bath area, Nat Forrest sat up and rubbed his head, and an ambulance's siren wailed in the background as all hell broke loose at the staid Tokyo Lawn Tennis Club.

CHAPTER 3

Captain "Tim" Kawamura of the Azabu Police Station sat at his desk clipping his fingernails. Seniority of some twenty-odd years had earned for him the privilege of avoiding weekend work most of the time. On Saturdays in the summer, however, everyone was eligible for duty to complement rosters depleted by vacations. He was not happy about things, but it was part of the job. The nail on the little finger of his left hand had still not grown back—it having been bitten off by a prostitute from Thailand during a routine raid on a Roppongi disco a month ago.

The call to the police station was registered at 11:42 A.M. The message was somewhat garbled—panic appeared to be in evidence—but the gist of the report indicated that a "respected Japanese" had been found very clean but very dead at the tennis club up the hill in the wealthy area of town. Kawamura put the fingernail clippers into the desk drawer, picked up the phone, and called his wife.

"I may not be home in an hour," Kawamura explained in his best "it's not my fault" voice.

Kawamura watched his assistant, Suzuki-san, pace back and forth with extreme agitation in front of his desk. Kawamura's wife was reminding Kawamura of his promise to take the two children to Tokyo Disneyland for the afternoon.

"I understand all that," said Kawamura into the phone, "but developments are not clear. We may have to delay it until tomorrow."

Kawamura's wife was lecturing on the theme of "promises made are debts unpaid" as Suzuki-san bit off the end of his pencil.

"Let's play it by ear," counseled Kawamura as he hung up the phone. Suzuki-san was twitching, giving every indication of going into a jumping-up-and-down routine.

"We must hurry," announced Suzuki-san, "it's a respected Japanese."

Kawamura picked up two pencils and a ballpoint pen from his desk. He rummaged around in the top drawer of the desk and found a relatively unused notepad.

"All Japanese," Kawamura explained to his assistant Suzuki-san, "are respected."

The two men walked from the Azabu Police Station and joined the overkill force of twenty-five law enforcement officers en route to the Tokyo Lawn Tennis Club. As Kawamura slid into the back seat of the lead patrol car, his thoughts were less on the hastily reported details of the death—drowned in a bath—than they were on the very real possibility that his investigations would involve entering the murky world of international citizens and relationships. And this particular club had more than its share of that kind of thing.

CHAPTER 4

The scene outside the club was typical of normal Saturday afternoons in the exclusive residential neighborhood. A recently disgraced political leader lived across the street, and this attracted a dozen or more press vehicles which were illegally parked along the narrow road.

Dodging and ducking members of the press were another dozen or so political leaders attempting to pay respects to their disgraced colleague and, perhaps more specifically, attempting to contain the damage potentially wrought by the disgraced one's further babbling in public. The political leaders' cars were also illegally parked.

In addition, two separate political demonstrations were taking place—one at the Chinese Embassy around the corner from the club, and the other at the Korean Embassy down the hill from the club. Wrongs, real *and* imagined, were being addressed by several hundred concerned citizens driving loudspeaker trucks or marching along the street carrying placards.

Compounding things was the presence of eight large police vans carrying national troopers assigned to the task of maintaining law and order amongst the demonstrators. The vans, camped next to the illegally parked vehicles, not only reduced normal traffic to one lane, they also contributed to the elements of chaos which would not be sorted out until well after sundown.

Captain Kawamura sat calmly in the back seat of his car as the driver twisted and turned his way through the hordes—at one point traveling several meters down the sidewalk in front of the hospital next to the club which, as luck would have it, was in the middle of visiting hours. Police captains were expected to be driven, although walking to the club would take half as much time as the car ride. An ambulance, stuck crossways in the street, was wailing away and generally contributing to the festivities. A normal Saturday in Tokyo, Kawamura mused.

Several club employees—the office manager, the court manager, and four female clerical staff members—stood in two columns at the entranceway as Kawamura's car bounced across the curbing and finally came to rest. Kawamura crawled out of the back seat, walked up the four broad steps, and briefly acknowledged the employees' bows with a brief nod of his head. The employees, Kawamura observed, were treating him with the kind of ingrained dignity more properly reserved for individuals in the Imperial Family—members of the club and frequent visitors. The gods, in all their wisdom, had at least contrived to arrange an Imperial absence on this particular day.

The clubhouse proper was a scene of barely controlled hysteria. Members in tennis outfits paced back and forth looking worried, frightened, and, in a few cases, angry. But surprisingly, and it was Suzuki-san who pointed this out, at least half the courts outside the large glass doors were occupied by people pounding away at their games— seemingly unaware, or at least unconcerned, about the reported developments in the locker room.

A dignified man, whose face looked vaguely familiar to Kawamura, walked up and introduced himself. He was the club president, he said, Tatsuo Morimoto. During the introductory bowing ceremonies, Kawamura remembered where he had seen the man. In the newspapers. Tatsuo Morimoto was a retired foreign service officer and former Japanese Ambassador to the United States. Kawamura held his last bow a beat longer than he would otherwise.

"I'm afraid we have a very sad development here," announced Morimoto at the conclusion of the ceremonies. Morimoto had contrived to produce a business card from the interior of his tennis costume.

"That's what I understand," said Kawamura. "Something about the bath, and apparently . . . ah, a member . . . "

"Very sad," confirmed Morimoto without moving but managing to look diplomatically sad. "Very sad indeed."

Kawamura repeated "very sad" and managed to duplicate the impression of sadness.

"But perhaps it would help if I could, ah, examine the area where the sadness occurred," explained Kawamura.

"Of course," responded Morimoto, suddenly adopting a businesslike attitude. "It's up the stairs in the locker room."

Kawamura followed Morimoto and a half-dozen Concerned Members up the circular staircase to the bath area. "Very sad" was murmured by the accompanying entourage.

The locker room was modern, air-conditioned, and equipped with all the niceties one expects in a first-class operation—towels, toothbrushes, spotless floors, hairdryers, and tatami flooring in the entranceway to the bath. A foreigner, naked and apparently in a traumatized state, gazed toward Kawamura with round and unfocused eyes as the entourage approached the bath.

"Is he all right?" Kawamura asked Morimoto with reference to the foreigner.

"We think so," answered Morimoto. "He was . . . shocked by discovering the, ah, sad problem."

Shig Manabe's body, formerly housing one of the nicest guys in the world, had now sunk completely under water. Only the toes stuck up above the crimson fluid. The court manager, who had greeted Kawamura on the steps outside the club, had managed to remove his necktie and beat the entourage to the bath area. He was now demonstrating his commitment to things by vigorously flourishing a mop around the floor.

"We think he slipped and cracked his head,"

explained Morimoto, as Kawamura studied the scene. "And that's why . . . "

"Tell him to stop that," said Kawamura abruptly. The court manager, not comfortable with outsiders giving directions, paused in his mopping chores and looked at the club president.

"Stop that," confirmed Morimoto.

"Has anybody touched anything here?" asked Kawamura.

The locker room denizens mumbled noncommittally.

"I touched the mop," replied the court manager after a moment. He had been spreading pink puddles around the floor next to the bath.

"Anything else?" asked Kawamura.

"Well," considered the court manager thoughtfully, "maybe just the towel." The court manager indicated a pile of obviously clean towels stacked neatly on a cabinet. "Shig, er, Manabe-san hadn't used his yet, and we're supposed to reduce the expense for laundry . . . " The court manager's comments trailed off.

Kawamura looked down at the body in the bath.

"We called an ambulance," explained Morimoto, "even before we called you. For some reason . . . "

"It's outside, still . . . stuck in traffic," said Kawamura interrupting. "Are you certain nothing else has been touched?"

No one answered.

"Sometimes the footing in the bath, getting in and out, can be dangerous. Particularly when ... "

President Morimoto's remarks were interrupted by the still-naked foreigner.

"I think there was a tennis racket on the floor. Next to the bath. At least, that's what I remember."

"A tennis racket?" Kawamura repeated, using the English pronunciation.

"Oh, that," said the court manager. "I gave it to . . . "

"Me," said a young man wearing a white shirt, polka-dot necktie, blue blazer, boxer shorts with red dots, calf-length socks, and no trousers. "And I gave it to . . . "

"Me," said a very tan, middle-aged man wearing jockey shorts and a spectacular bandage on his elbow. "And I gave it to . . . "

"Me," said a dapper man wearing a cravat under his paisley shirt. "And I gave it to . . . "

"Me," said a gray-haired gentleman—the other half of the now defunct Silver Foxes. "And I put it back in the rack where tennis rackets belong. Water ruins the gut strings."

Kawamura stared at the group surrounding him. A basic precept taught in all courses on detection dictated that private feelings and personal emotions had no place in the analytical process. Kawamura turned to his assistant, Suzuki-san.

"Get the damn racket, be careful with it, and seal it."

"What could be so important about the racket?" asked Morimoto. "Slipping in the bath . . . "

"I have no idea what's important about the racket," answered Kawamura. "But simple observation, even without the ambulance people, indicates that your friend here suffered from a . . . different problem."

"Different problem?"

"Different problem. The rim of the bath is horizontal. Your friend died as the result of a vertical blow . . . which nearly split his head lengthwise."

The locker room denizens and Kawamura were staring at what used to be one of the nicest guys in the world—now in water turning almost purple—as the white-coated ambulance personnel bounded into the room.

CHAPTER 5

The first couple of hours after the discovery of a tragic death can be both frustrating and rewarding. On the one hand, there are the complications brought about by confusion, shock, and perhaps hysteria. Even sealing off the scene of events can be difficult with random medical technicians and investigating officers shuffling about their tasks. More hard evidence is destroyed at this time than is generally appreciated.

On the other hand, the questioning of potential

witnesses during the first two hours after a tragedy often brings answers that have not been reworked, polished, or enhanced. Kawamura's practice had always been to begin taking statements immediately.

Normally Kawamura would have established himself as close as possible to the scene of the event so that witnesses could demonstrate sightlines and distances with some degree of accuracy. In this case however, the chaos brought about by removing the body, draining the bath, scrubbing the floor, and more specifically, dealing with hot and sweating members demanding access to their lockers was something to be avoided. Instead, Kawamura borrowed the manager's office downstairs.

An immediate problem facing Kawamura was the fact that he wasn't certain what he was investigating. Presumably the wound on the top of Shig Manabe's head *could* have been caused by the rim of the tub, but only if Manabe was whirling on his toes as he entered the bath. And Manabe didn't seem to be the type to execute the graceful pirouettes of a ballet dancer. To be certain of his suspicions, Kawamura would have to wait for the preliminary findings from the coroner.

One thing *was* certain, however. People seemed to like the victim. Kawamura first interviewed Nat Forrest, the Discoverer of the Body. Fortunately, someone had persuaded Forrest to put on some clothes—he now wore a tennis shirt, shorts, and a sock on his left foot—but he was still obviously dazed by the experience.

Forrest's English was rapid and a little out of control, but Kawamura managed to discern that (a) Forrest had stepped into the bath with his right foot before he noticed Manabe's condition, (b) Forrest, without his glasses, didn't see anyone enter or leave the bath area, and (c) Forrest, being a relatively new member of the club, didn't really know anyone very well anyway. He considered Manabe to be "one of the nicest people in the world" because he would occasionally play with him. But Nat Forrest also confirmed that he did not play with Shig Manabe that day.

Out of respect for seniority, Kawamura next interviewed the club president, former Ambassador Morimoto. The former ambassador answered all questions precisely and in measured tones. Yes, there were about a dozen people in the locker room when Shig's body was discovered. Yes, the ambassador was one of those people. No, nothing seemed unusual or different. Yes, more people could have roamed in or out of the locker room during the time in question. No, from where he was standing—in front of his locker taking off his street clothes—he could not see into the bath area. No, he could not think of any reason on earth why anyone would want to harm Shig Manabe. Yes, Manabe had been a member of the club for over thirty years. No, he did not think strangers or nonmembers could have entered the locker room. Yes, Shig Manabe was one of the most decent human beings he'd ever met.

"Are you ruling out an accident?" asked Morimoto at the conclusion of the interview.

"Frankly, sir," replied Kawamura, "I'm not ruling out anything."

The rediscoverer of the body, Mr. Lee Kim, told Captain Kawamura that he had gone into the bath area to get a bucket of water to splash on Nat Forrest. According to Kim, Forrest had been "acting crazy" and Kim thought hot water in the face might bring him to his senses.

"I filled the bucket from the bath, turned around to leave," reported Kim, "then my brain realized what my eyes had just seen. Shig underwater."

"Didn't you notice the water was slightly . . . dark?" asked Kawamura.

"My eyes saw it, but my brain didn't . . ."

"I understand. Then what did you do?"

Kim squinted in concentration.

"I went back out to the locker room and announced that Shig was in trouble," answered Kim, still squinting.

"What did you do with the bucket of water?"

"Poured it back into the tub," said Kim, now wide-eyed.

The next series of interviews revealed very little beyond what was already known. The man in the white shirt, polka-dot tie, blue blazer, and now wearing trousers—Yamaguchi by name—explained that Manabe had just entered the bath area as he was leaving the bath. An exact time could not be ascertained, but Yamaguchi mentioned that he noticed it was "about twenty after eleven" when he was dressing. To demonstrate the reason for his observation, Yamaguchi pointed to his gold Rolex watch. Accepting, then passing on Manabe's tennis racket to someone else, seemed perfectly normal in a club where tennis rackets abound.

"I would like to say a final thing," mentioned Yamaguchi. "You should know that Manabe-san is, er, was, one of the nicest people I've ever met."

The man Kawamura first met wearing jockey shorts and a spectacular bandage on his elbow was now dressed in a complete tennis outfit upon which the word "Nike" appeared on every conceivable surface—from shoes to headband. He was, he said, distantly related to Manabe—his grandfather had married Manabe's father's cousin. Kawamura and the man could not work out the exact relationship, but that was frequently the way in Japan. The man went on to explain that of all his relatives, no matter how distant, Shig Manabe was the warmest and most genuine.

Theodore Bitman, originally from Salt Lake City, Utah, had also been in the locker room at the approximate time of Shig's death. Bitman, it developed, had been something of a competitor of Shig's—at least in business. Bitman arrived in Japan in 1963 as a Mormon missionary. He was fluent in Japanese, and at some point after the Tokyo Olympics in 1964, he decided to broaden his horizons and serve both the god of conversion *and* the god of mammon. Bitman was a well-known commentator on Japanese television regarding "things foreign," but he also ran a flourishing business exporting pearls and jewelry from Japan to the United States. Bitman Pearls were not as well-known as Mikimoto Pearls, but at least in Japan the company ranked higher in status than Manabe's company.

"He was one of the most trustworthy individuals I've ever known in business," announced Bitman during the interview with Kawamura.

"But you were rivals," said Kawamura.

"Makes no difference," answered Bitman. "The market is the world. We each just had a little part of it."

Bitman did not notice anything unusual in the locker room. He was changing into his tennis gear when "Forrest ran screaming from the bath." His role in the matter was confined to attempting to calm Forrest before "another foreigner made an ass of himself" in front of the Japanese.

The interview with the dapper man wearing a cravat under his paisley shirt produced the same results. Shig Manabe was one of the nicest guys in the world, nothing seemed unusual in the locker room, and passing a tennis racket along from one person to another was the "most natural thing in the world." The dapper man, who had obviously spent a great deal of time in the States, tended to amplify his remarks with random words in English—a habit Kawamura found irritating.

The court manager, who had met Kawamura on the steps at the entrance to the club, and who had later been mopping up the area around the bath, was either "checking the practice board," "settling a dispute regarding court usage," or "confirming tournament standings in the clubhouse" when the nasty business was occurring. He had been nowhere near the locker room at the time.

The most interesting interview of those deemed to have been in the locker room at the time of Manabe's death was the last one. Takashi Sakai was the other half of the now defunct Silver Foxes partnership. A robust and somewhat aggressive man, Sakai was at sixty-eight the same age as Manabe. The two of them had spent their early grade-school years together in Yokohama. They had been playing tennis together off and on for nearly fifty years

"Nice man? That bastard would call foot faults on *himself*," Sakai stated. "And the fool would always give the benefit of the doubt on line calls to our opponents."

"I gather you knew him well," suggested Kawamura.

"Knew him well? All my life. That whoremaster's son would never stand up and fight for himself."

"But if you . . . "

"He always swayed with the wind. He thought that was the way to survive," amplified Sakai.

"But if you . . . "

"He'd hit a killer shot, and that peddler's dog would apologize to our opponents."

"But if you . . . "

"He once walked away from a fight when someone said something about his American wife. I would have clobbered the pig-brain for saying that, even though I hate Americans."

"Did you and Manabe-san argue a lot?" asked Kawamura.

"Argue a lot? Of course. Today, for example, he didn't chase a single lob. That blowfish smoked too much. We lost because of him."

Kawamura and Sakai stared at each other across the desk.

"To answer your previous question," said Sakai at last. "No, I didn't notice a thing in the locker room."

"Nothing?"

"Nothing. And to answer the question you didn't ask, if anyone really wanted to kill him, it would probably be me."

Kawamura and Sakai stared at each other. Finally Sakai turned his head and looked out the manager's window at the nearly deserted courts.

Then the remaining Silver Fox took off his thick glasses, put his head down on the desk, and began to cry.

CHAPTER 6

Weekend evenings at the Tokyo Lawn Tennis Club were usually quite relaxed. Anywhere from seventy-five to a hundred members would normally sit around, discuss the day's games, tell funny stories, eat, and quench thirsts developed as the result of hours spent chasing around on the courts. To put this in perspective, although the club boasted some of the top Japanese and foreign players in the country, more bottles of beer were typically consumed annually than cans of tennis balls.

On this Saturday evening, however, there was nothing but gloom. A couple-dozen members sat quietly, watched Captain Kawamura's methodical investigators going through their routines, and discussed Shig. Dusk had emptied the ten outdoor clay courts.

Kawamura could feel the awkwardness and tension as he walked around watching his men take measurements and photograph every conceivable feature in the clubhouse. Kawamura secretly knew that all the measurements and photographs in the world could not possibly determine what happened upstairs in the locker room, but investigative routine was well spelled out in the manual, and his superiors would expect to see the results of these labors in the file.

A foreigner, speaking English with a heavy French accent, broke the ice.

"Please, *monsieur l'inspecteur,* if you could tell what it is that happened to Manabe-san? He was a friend to all of us. "

The other members silently looked at Kawamura.

"I am not a, mesher lonspec . . . ah," replied Kawamura crisply in English, "I am only a police captain."

"Then, *mon capitaine,* what was the circumstance in the bath?"

The other members silently looked at Kawamura.

"Our investigations are still . . . continuing," answered Kawamura.

To the Japanese members he added, in Japanese: "We have no clear idea what happened."

The other members silently looked at Kawamura.

"Manabe-san was a very nice man," said one of the Japanese members after a moment.

CHAPTER 7

"Nobody can be that nice," announced Kawamura's assistant, Suzuki-san.

Kawamura and Suzuki-san were eating dinner at a Chinese restaurant in the Azabu Juban section of Tokyo—down the hill from the tennis club and a good three kilometers from the police station. There was merit in collecting thoughts before returning to bureaucratic demands at headquarters. Besides, neither man had eaten since breakfast.

"I mean, I worry about people who are always thought to be nice. There's usually something wrong."

Kawamura looked at his assistant. Suzuki-san, now a sergeant, was respected more for his loyalty than his brainpower. At forty, Suzuki-san had decided that the best way to deal with a balding head was to shave it to the skin. That, plus a tendency to wear the same blue serge suit summer and winter, set him apart from the usual upwardly mobile staff on the force.

"Why do you say that?" asked Kawamura between mouthfuls of dumplings.

"My wife's uncle," answered Suzuki-san, who

was working on a bowl of noodles festooned with slices of pink pork. "He was also very nice. Quiet. Respectful. He went to the shrines on all holidays. Everybody liked him. He also cut up my wife's aunt into little pieces and fed her to the birds in a park near Ueno Zoo. It surprised everybody."

Kawamura set aside the last dumpling on his plate.

"I hate going to that park now. When the birds . . ."

"Never mind," interrupted Kawamura. "What did you learn from the staff at the club?"

"Mrs. Moto, head of the kitchen, said Shig Manabe would often forget to pay his bill. He would leave town for months with an outstanding debit."

"That's hardly grounds for . . . whatever happened to him."

"And the young waitresses. He would find out their home phone numbers, call them, and request that they visit him at his apartment."

"Well," said Kawamura, "I guess he *was* friendly, but still that's not a motive for . . ."

"The court manager said that Manabe-san and his regular tennis partner . . ."

"Sakai."

"Sakai. They would have tremendous fights. About their tennis games, I guess."

"I interviewed Sakai-san," said Kawamura, "but I think he felt closer to Manabe than maybe even he realizes."

"Also, the office manager told me that Manabe and the foreigner who talks perfect Japanese had a big problem. Something about business."

"Bitman? I talked to him."

"Yes, Bitman. Theodore Bitman. We sometimes see him on television. Manabe once sued him."

Kawamura watched the waitress clearing away their plates. In his early days on the police force, Kawamura was assigned to the "illegal immigrant" detail. Picking up people like the waitress, visitors who overstayed their tourist visas merely to work, was like spreading a net in a school of fish. This woman, an Oriental lady, could not even understand the Japanese for "more beer."

"We'd better investigate that lawsuit," said Kawamura. "Bitman told me that he had great respect for Manabe."

The waitress delivered two cups of Chinese tea, which Suzuki-san waved away—pointing to the empty beer bottles and holding up two fingers.

"And the most unusual thing," continued Suzuki-san, "was what the head groundsman told me."

"The head groundsman? What does he do?"

"Sweeps the courts. But he knows everything that goes on. He's been there since the war."

"What did he say?"

"He said that Manabe and the fancy man . . . "

"The fancy man?" asked Kawamura.

"The fancy man. He was wearing a handker-chief around his neck today . . . "

"Ah, yes," said Kawamura. "He was one of those in the locker room. Paisley shirt."

"Fruit-salad shirt. His name is Kimura. And the groundsman told me that one morning he and Manabe were fighting each other and rolling around on the clay courts. The groundsman had to break them up."

"Fighting? I didn't think Manabe *ever* fought. When was this?"

"Fifteen years ago," answered Suzuki-san. "And ever since then, Manabe and Kimura won't even play on courts that are next to each other."

Kawamura watched the waitress deliver four bottles of beer. Clearly, there was a communication problem.

"Well, there's one good thing," said Kawamura at last. "Because the . . . ah . . . problem took place in the men's locker room, we can rule out half the people who were there today."

"Women? No, we can't," answered Suzuki-san. "Our people found a cigarette with lipstick on the butt in the men's toilet next to the bath."

"Are you serious?"

"Serious. And smoking isn't even allowed up there."

Kawamura sighed and picked up the check.

"Let's go back to the station. I'd like nothing better than to learn from the coroner's office that Manabe, for reasons of his own, dove head-first into that bath."

A long and complicated discussion ensued with the manager of the Chinese restaurant regarding two of the last four beers that had been served during the meal.

CHAPTER 8

The Azabu Police Station, located in the heart of the Roppongi entertainment district, is like any major city police station in the world. Drunks, foreigners, criminals, lost souls, and Concerned Citizens wandered or were ushered in and out the main entrance. Patrolmen in uniforms—intent on assignments—bumped into each other as they rushed up and down the narrow stairs.

Activity on Saturday nights in the summer was always heavier than usual. Kawamura and Suzuki-san passed a man whose car had tipped over in the main Roppongi intersection, a wedding party of twenty or twenty-five people who were lost and should have been in Shibuya, a woman in jeans who claimed that her diamonds and pearls had been stolen in the Hard Rock Cafe, and seven Iranians who could not understand why selling baubles on the sidewalk outside the police station was not permitted. Kawamura even caught a glimpse of the prostitute from Thailand who had bitten off his little fingernail.

Upon reaching his third-floor office, Kawamura was informed that Police Chief Arai had made an unusual Saturday-night visit to the station, and that he requested Kawamura's presence in his office "the very instant" he walked in the door.

Kawamura nodded agreement, looked at the phone messages on his desk, thought about calling his wife, then decided to go up the one flight of stairs and see Arai. There were, Kawamura thought, easier ways to earn a living.

Police Chief Arai was a force to be reckoned with. Not only was he in command of the Azabu Police Department—a position of power and authority—he was a dynamo personally. He would intimidate people if he were a janitor.

"Where the hell have you been?" greeted Arai warmly as Kawamura entered the office. "The international and diplomatic world is coming to an end, and you disappear."

"We just had dinner and . . . "

"Had *dinner*? Do you realize what happened at the Tokyo Lawn Tennis Club?"

"Of course, or I think so. That's where I've been since . . . "

"Six or seven foreign ambassadors are members," counseled Arai, "a former ambassador to the United States is the president, and . . . "

Arai made head-jerking motions with his head over his shoulder.

"The Imperial Family?" suggested Kawamura helpfully.

Arai nearly jumped out of his chair.

"Don't even *say* that. Protocol."

"Yes, but . . . "

"And you're out having dinner. Do you realize the implications?"

"Yes, or no. I mean, I've been investigating . . . "

"Do you realize it was cold-blooded murder? A respected Japanese who was also an international citizen?"

"We're not sure of that yet. It could have been an accident and . . . "

Police Chief Arai slammed his hand on the desk, causing papers, pens, and knickknacks to bounce and rattle.

"You must be a complete idiot," explained Arai. "Hey, you, tell him."

Arai nodded toward the corner of his office. A man Kawamura had not noticed before sat cowering in his chair. He wore a gray rumpled suit, a gray rumpled necktie, and had gray rumpled hair.

"Er, ah, my name is Chokei, and I . . . "

"Cut the goddam introductions," counseled Arai. "Tell him what the hell you think."

"Er, ah, my office . . . the coroner's office . . . thinks the fatal blow to the head was most probably made by the tennis racket which was submitted as evidence. The configuration of the rim and the, ah, string-channels is consistent with . . . "

"See?" amplified Arai for Kawamura. "Unless you can demonstrate that your victim committed suicide by pounding himself over the head . . . "

"Are there fingerprints?" Kawamura asked Chokei.

"Not really. The grip is cloth, designed to absorb perspiration, and . . . "

"Don't get fancy, Kawamura, your job is to find out who did it," recommended Arai.

" . . . and the residual tissue and blood traces match those of the . . . "

"Stop that. Both of you," advised Arai. "Your job is to find out who did it. How many times do I have to tell you?"

Kawamura rose and began to back out of the room.

"Your input," he said, "is always very valuable, Chief Arai."

Kawamura and Chokei left Arai's office together.

"Is it always like this?" asked Chokei. "I mean, working here?"

"In a way, yes," answered Kawamura. "But it's sometimes worse."

The two men began to descend the stairs.

"We think the killer was right-handed. The right side of the racket's rim was the leading edge . . . "

"Thanks," said Kawamura.

"If you need more help . . . "

"I appreciate it, Chokei-san."

The two men parted on the third floor—Chokei quickly blending into the gray background and, presumably, down the gray stairs and out into the gray night. Kawamura never saw him again, but that's just as well. Kawamura was already in bed when he realized that tennis rackets don't have right and left sides.

CHAPTER 9

Sunday morning was bright and sunny, and at 9:00 A.M. it showed every indication of becoming a very warm day. Japan's late spring-early summer rainy season was officially over and the populace was now in for two months of baking heat.

Captain Kawamura and Sergeant Suzuki, wearing suits and ties, walked up the four broad steps to the entrance of the tennis club.

"I just want to observe the normal flow of things," said Kawamura to Suzuki. "Get a feel for things."

"We should have worn tennis outfits," said Suzuki-san, who was already sweating profusely in his blue serge suit.

"Requesting a duty-shift in short pants would probably cause Chief Arai to feed *us* to the birds out by the zoo."

The temperature inside the entrance lobby was slightly lower, but not much. To the right, behind a chest-high counter, was the manager's office. To the left, the circular stairway up to the men's and women's locker rooms. Straight ahead were large wooden doors leading to the clubhouse proper. Immediately to the right of the wooden doors was a reception desk. The lady rose from her seat behind the desk and stood at attention.

"Please don't stand for us," said Kawamura gently.

The lady obediently sat.

"I would imagine you see nearly everyone who comes in or goes out."

"I think so," said the lady, who proceeded to point out a sign-in book near the wooden doors. "Everyone, including guests, must sign the book when they arrive."

Kawamura looked through the names, Japanese and foreign, signed in yesterday. There were over two hundred.

"Some people stay all day," added the lady, "and some only stay for a few hours."

"Is Manabe-san's name here?"

The lady looked embarrassed.

"It's not there," said the lady after a moment. "Manabe was a very nice man, but some of the older members didn't like to always sign the book."

The lady picked up a piece of paper from her desk and showed it to Kawamura.

"In those cases, I try to write down their names anyway."

On the paper, neatly written, was Manabe's name. There were also a dozen other names, presumably older members, on the list.

"You are very efficient," said Kawamura, smiling kindly.

The lady blushed ever so slightly. Kawamura

turned and looked at the spiral stairway to the second-floor locker rooms. One man had just come through the wooden doors and the club-house proper and was now bounding up the stairway. He passed two ladies coming down the stairway.

"Did you notice Manabe-san going up to the locker room yesterday?"

"No," said the lady hesitating briefly. "Some-times it gets very busy in here. And sometimes . . . if I have to step away from my desk for a moment . . . it's difficult to . . . "

"I understand," said Kawamura softly. "One can't sit here for an entire eight hours."

The lady smiled. It was a relief to know that the policeman understood.

Kawamura and Suzuki-san opened the wooden doors and entered the clubhouse.

"In theory, we have over two hundred members from yesterday as suspects," said Kawamura, "and as far as we know, a million or more people who could have walked in from the street."

All ten courts were already occupied, most with foursomes. Another fifty or sixty people were sitting, talking, or eating breakfast. The mood did not appear to be cheerful, but Kawamura had never been in the clubhouse under normal cir-cumstances and couldn't really judge.

The club president, former Ambassador Morimoto, had just come in from the courts. He even managed to sweat with control and a certain elegance. He promised to join Kawamura after getting a cool drink. Suzuki-san wandered out to courtside and began to talk to the groundsmen there.

Morimoto eventually joined Kawamura at a table and chairs in a relatively deserted area of the clubhouse.

"The club office tells me we finally located Manabe-san's wife in New York," announced Morimoto as he sat and patted his brow with a towel. Kawamura observed that the former ambassador's hair wasn't even mussed. "And she'll get to Japan as soon as possible. Probably tomorrow," Morimoto added.

"I must tell you that the, ah, tragedy is even worse than you might think," said Kawamura. "We are convinced Manabe-san was murdered, and the murder weapon is his tennis racket."

Morimoto stared at Kawamura for a moment, then shifted his eyes to the ceiling and the general direction of the locker room. Morimoto shook his head slowly, as if he couldn't believe it, then looked back at Kawamura.

"I can't believe it," said Morimoto.

"We can't argue with the physical evidence, no matter how unlikely the event might seem."

"I understand. What other . . . evidence do you have?"

"You mean suspects? None, I'm afraid, but that's where you can help us perhaps."

Morimoto shifted slightly in his chair.

"As president of this club," Morimoto said after taking a deep breath, "I have a responsibility to the individual members. I'm not certain I can divulge confidences that might prove to be harmful to the individual members."

"With all due respect, sir, as president of this club there's also a responsibility to prevent the harmful occurrence of members being killed in the bath."

It may have been Kawamura's imagination, but the former ambassador's façade of confidence cracked slightly—something about the little lines appearing at the corners of the eyes.

"How long have you been a policeman, Lieutenant Kawaguchi?"

"I'm a captain, sir, and the name is Kawamura. I've been a policemen for twenty-three years, seven months, and fourteen days."

Morimoto stared at Kawamura.

"The Azabu Police Station?" said Morimoto at last. "I believe your boss is Chief Sakakibara."

"No sir, Chief Sakakibara retired three years ago. The chief is now Arai."

"Ah yes," said Morimoto, "Chief Arai . . . the peasant from Hokkaido."

Kawamura made no comment.

"Well," said Morimoto, "you are doing your job. What do you want to know?"

"It's pretty simple, really," said Kawamura. "The crime doesn't seem to be complicated, well thought-out, or something planned in advance. Too many things could go wrong. Who would have hated Manabe-san enough to suddenly come up and on the spur of the moment kill him?"

"Everyone liked Manabe. He was one of our most popular members . . . "

"Obviously someone didn't like him."

"That's a point," conceded Morimoto. "Maybe in the heat of the moment, because of a tennis game . . . ," Morimoto's voice trailed off.

"His partner? Sakai-san?"

Morimoto dabbed his forehead with the towel.

"I would have thought that would be obvious," he said at the conclusion of the dabbing.

"Really?" said Kawamura. "They seem to have been friends for a long time. Most of their lives. They certainly played a lot of tennis together."

Morimoto ordered another drink from a passing waitress, Kawamura asked for coffee.

"No one else would play tennis with Sakai. He is . . . a difficult man."

"Really?"

"He was an early member of the club," explained Morimoto. "I'm not certain he would pass the entrance interview today. He does not represent the type of 'international member' we strive for currently."

"But he played tennis with Manabe-san, he was . . . an international character, and Manabe's wife was American."

"Sakai hates Americans," said Morimoto, "and as I said, no one else would play with him."

The waitress delivered a tall glass of iced juice for Morimoto and a cup of coffee for Kawamura.

"What about the staff here?" asked Kawamura after the waitress had left. "Were there indications that Manabe-san may have . . . tried to be too friendly with the staff? The female staff, that is?

Morimoto gave an unambassadorial snort.

"That kind of thing is unthinkable."

"Do women ever go into the men's locker room?" asked Kawamura.

"Women? In the men's locker room? Never. Why?

"We found a cigarette butt in an ashtray in the men's toilet next to bath. There was lipstick on the butt."

"That's impossible," said Morimoto. "Women can't go in the men's locker room. And anyway, smoking is prohibited up there."

"We can't argue with physical evidence," Kawamura remarked. "But I can't imagine a woman being strong enough to do . . . what was done to Manabe-san."

Outside on court number one, a solidly built young lady slowly tossed a ball into the air, then delivered a serve with sufficient force to have split Shig Manabe down to his socks.

"What was Manabe-san's relationship with a man named Kimura?" Kawamura asked. "He was in the locker room yesterday, and one of the staff told us that he and Manabe once had knock-down, roll-around fight out on the courts."

"Which member of the staff told you that?" asked Morimoto quickly.

Kawamura took a sip of his coffee.

"I'm not sure that's important," he answered. "What was their relationship?"

"This is a private club, and our staff shouldn't be . . . "

"I appreciate all that," said Kawamura, "but a murder occurred in this private club. What was their relationship?"

"Kimura used to work for Manabe. That was years ago. Kimura used to travel back and forth to the States from Japan. After a while, they had some . . . disagreement about the business. That was all."

"A fight? And then not even playing next to each other for fifteen years?"

"Memories, particularly in love and business, are long," replied the Tokyo Lawn Tennis Club president.

"Long enough to commit murder?"

"Ridiculous," said Morimoto. "Murder would have occurred at the time of the fight, not now. What did Kimura say when you spoke to him?"

"He said Manabe was the nicest guy in the world."

"See? That proves it."

Kawamura wasn't sure what it proved. Morimoto was looking over his shoulder at three men who were standing by the glass doors obviously waiting to go out and play.

"I'm afraid I must excuse myself," said Morimoto.

"I understand that, sir, but I would like to ask you about Manabe-san's relationship with a man named Bitman."

"Theodore Bitman? He's not Japanese."

"I understand that, but . . . "

"Non-Japanese tend to come and go regularly," said Morimoto.

"Bitman has been in Japan since 1963."

"Then I suggest you speak to him directly," said Morimoto rising from his chair and joining his friends for another game.

CHAPTER 10

Kawamura and Suzuki-san stood looking down at the bath. Everything had been cleaned and there were no traces of the horror of the previous day. People came and went from the locker room, and the showers were frequently used, but no one had deemed it proper to use the bath.

"I can't help but think we're just roaming around aimlessly," said Suzuki-san.

"You're probably right. Did you find out anything new?"

"Not really," replied Suzuki-san. "But I confirmed that Manabe had a . . . very strong taste for female company. Not just for the waitresses. Also for some of the wives of the members."

"Hmm," observed Kawamura. "Any names?"

"Not yet. The staff, of course, notices all of that. But they are . . . slow to say anything."

"I can imagine that. Morimoto doesn't like the idea of the staff talking to outsiders."

Kawamura and Suzuki walked to the entrance of the men's locker room. Women reaching the top of the circular stairway would turn right to the women's locker room, men would turn left. It was possible to imagine a woman entering the men's locker room and quickly ducking to the left into the toilet area, but it would depend on whether or not anyone from the rows of lockers happened to be looking in that direction. Getting from the toilet area into the bath, however, would involve a dash through open space. Unless the locker room was deserted, that would be impossible.

"Are we certain that there was lipstick on that cigarette butt?" asked Kawamura.

"Certain," replied Suzuki-san. "Estée Lauder Burnt Orange Flame, in fact. And the cigarette was a Mild Seven—the most popular brand in Japan."

"Wonderful," said Kawamura after a moment.

Kawamura and Suzuki-san stood at the top of the stairs. An enormous, stuffed elk head was inexplicably mounted on the wall near the locker room entrances.

"It would be nice if that creature could talk," said Suzuki-san, looking at the elk head.

"It would probably only complicate things," said Kawamura. "Anyway, tomorrow we should pay a visit to Mr. Theodore Bitman and find out why Manabe sued him. And we should pay a call on your friend in the fruit-salad shirt, Kimura-san. If he used to work for Manabe, their fight on the courts might have had something to do with that."

"What about Sakai?"

"I guess we should talk to him again, too," said Kawamura. "It seems that Morimoto thinks he's a likely suspect. A fight over the damn game, or something like that."

Kawamura and Suzuki-san began to walk slowly down the circular staircase. Halfway down, they met the foreigner with the heavy French accent who was climbing the steps in his street clothes.

"Ah, *mon capitaine,*" said the Frenchman, "the situation has some new difficulties, no?"

"The situation is the same for Manabe-san. The situation for the rest of us is that we know now he was murdered."

"We have the saying in my country, *mon capitaine.* It is *cherchez la femme.*"

"Thank you," said Kawamura.

The Frenchman continued up the stairs.

"What did he say?" asked Suzuki-san.

"I have no idea," answered Kawamura. "We'll look it up when we get back to the station."

CHAPTER 11

On the Saturday night his partner died, the remaining Silver Fox got very drunk. Deciding against changing in the locker room, and after going through the ordeal of the interview with the policeman, Sakai walked out of the club in his tennis clothes and took a subway to his apartment in the Ueno section of Tokyo.

Sakai had purchased smaller quarters after his wife died, and he was perfectly content with the one large dining-living-sleeping room and the kitchenette. He drank the remaining third of a saké bottle as he took a shower.

He dressed and decided that a yakitori meal would be just right. Across the narrow street from his apartment, and down past the pachinko parlor, was a place he visited two or three times a month.

Sakai had two beers quickly before the first pieces of roasted chicken were presented. Sakai maintained the pace. By the time the meal was finished—finished as far as the proprietors were concerned—he had driven away a young couple seated next to him, sent a waitress to the back room in tears, and lectured an elderly man on the stupidity of trying to eat gizzards without teeth.

Sakai reluctantly left the restaurant before the dessert course, and lurched around the corner to a small snack shop were he kept a bottle of Suntory whiskey. He sat on his favorite stool in the corner and took off his shoes. Other patrons amiably chatted, read comic books, or watched television. Had anyone been paying particular attention, they would have noticed that Sakai was talking to himself more than usual as he worked his way through his bottle.

The televised tennis match from Wimbledon

sent Sakai over the edge. His shouts did not result in a change in channels, but they did result in the wife of the snack shop owner agreeing to walk Sakai home.

Sakai remembered pouring himself a drink when he got home, and he remembered turning on the television to watch the same tennis match, but he only vaguely recalled thinking about Shig— and again breaking into tears. Twice in one day.

Sakai woke up fully dressed sometime late Sunday morning, collected the morning paper outside his front door, scanned the paper for news of what happened at the tennis club, had another drink, took off his clothes, and went back to sleep.

The pounding, at first, reminded Sakai of drums. He rolled over, but the pounding would not go away. For a moment, he thought the sound had something to do with the thumping in his head.

He opened his eyes, and noticed that the light coming from the one window in the room was very faint. It was either early in the morning or late in the afternoon.

The pounding continued. Sakai sat up and looked at his watch. Late in the afternoon.

"Just a minute," Sakai yelled. Clearly someone was at the door.

Getting up and moving about for the first moment or so is probably more difficult for active athletes than for more retiring folks. Bumps, minor sprains, inflamed tendons, and bruised muscles scream in protest. Sunday, almost dark,

Sakai now realized, and who the hell would be visiting me now?

Sakai limped to the door and opened it. Two blue-suited, official-looking men with serious expressions stared at him.

"Police?" asked Sakai without thinking.

The man with the shortest hair grunted something in reply, and the two men pushed their way into the room.

Something was wrong. One man picked up Sakai's trousers from the floor and removed the belt. These guys are past retirement age for policemen, Sakai suddenly thought.

"Who *are* you?" Sakai asked, recognizing panic in his own voice.

The man with the shortest hair grabbed Sakai by the arm, twisted it behind him, and clamped a very dry and rough hand over his mouth. He began to drag Sakai to the kitchenette. Sakai's tennis activities had kept him in reasonably good shape, and the struggle was fairly even for a few moments. But the other man walked up and calmly punched Sakai in the stomach. Sakai felt his insides tear apart.

Through a fog, Sakai saw the other man drag a chair into the kitchenette.

"This should do," said the other man. The other man then punched Sakai in the stomach one more time.

The man with the shortest hair tossed the end of the belt over a water pipe running across the ceiling in the kitchenette.

To give him credit, Sakai put up a decent struggle. But there were two of them. And they knew what they were doing. Sakai tried to yell "No!" but it all happened so quickly. The man with the shortest hair let go of him, and before the choking red curtain overwhelmed Sakai, his last conscious thought was that the chair had tipped over down on the floor.

The two men watched Sakai's body slowly swing back and forth for a moment, then walked quietly to the door of the apartment. The man with the shortest hair reached a gloved hand inside the door and onto the doorknob lock button before gently closing the door.

CHAPTER 12

Kawamura and his wife sat on the floor around the low table in their living room. The two children, a boy and a girl, each occupied one of the two bedrooms in the apartment. Rock music, separate and competing, boomed from each room.

"Of course they were disappointed," said Noriko Kawamura. "We've been promising them a trip to Disneyland for months."

"I apologize, but this, ah, new case, requires immediate attention."

"Remember, their school summer vacation is only a few weeks, and . . . "

"I know, I know," said Kawamura, holding up his glass as his wife poured beer from the bottle, "a promise made is a debt unpaid. When this is over, I'll be able to take a few days off."

"Is it a difficult case?"

Kawamura never discussed the details of his police work with his wife for various reasons. For example, he explained the loss of his little fingernail by saying he caught it in the car door. To tell the absolute truth, and to spread the anguish of the three-week waiting period after the test for HIV to his family, was too much. He did take the entire family out to dinner on the evening the test results came back negative, and explained his jubilation as being the result of a meritorious citation.

But Noriko was level-headed and always displayed common sense. Talking in general about his work, or at least the puzzles in his work, would often develop a fresh and neutral point of view.

"Someone killed a man without any enemies at a tennis club," said Kawamura.

"There is no one without enemies."

"Well, that's what we'll probably find out, but in the meantime it seems more like a sudden crime of passion."

"I would think there are better places to kill someone than in a place with all kinds of people around," said Noriko as she rose and began to pick up the dirty dishes on the table.

"That's why we think it's probably a sudden crime of passion."

"Or," said Noriko over her shoulder as she took the dishes into the small kitchen, "it was done to prove something about the tennis club."

Kawamura was still staring at the blank television screen when Noriko returned to the living room.

"If you don't mind," she said, "I'd like to go to bed early. I'm exhausted. Shall I prepare your bath?"

"Ah, no, I think I'll just take a shower tonight. What did you do today?" asked Kawamura.

"Took the kids to Ueno Zoo."

"Did you feed the birds?"

"Yes," said Noriko to her husband the detective, "how did you know?"

CHAPTER 13

The Monday morning meeting in Chief Arai's office did not go smoothly. The morning papers had reported briefly on the discovery of a respected international Japanese businessman dead in the bath at the Tokyo Lawn Tennis Club. But all knew this was the relative calm before a publicity storm since the evening papers would certainly tumble to the truth.

"And that's all you plan to do?" bellowed the police chief. "Interview people and take fancy statements?"

"Well, we have to establish a motive . . . "

"Establish a motive?" roared Arai. "Somebody walked into the bath and hit your man over the head. Find out who did it."

"That's a good point, sir," said Kawamura. He and Suzuki-san rose from their chairs. "We had better get to it right away."

"And no dinner until you make somebody confess," whooped Arai as Kawamura and Suzuki-san left the office.

"That doesn't mean lunch, does it?" asked Suzuki-san as they walked down to the third floor.

The plan for the day involved setting up an appointment and meeting with Theodore Bitman to discuss his business situation and the reported lawsuit filed by Manabe-san against him. Research on the lawsuit was assigned to one of the younger members of the Azabu Police Department staff. Official channels do not always exist in Japan between the police departments and various government agencies, but in all cases it's relatively simple to obtain information. All it would take in this case is to find someone with a relative, classmate, neighbor, or friend with a relative, classmate, neighbor, or friend in the Ministry of

Justice. The process could be accomplished in half a day.

The next meeting was to be with Kimura-san, apparently a former employee of Manabe's and certainly a man with enough bottled-up passion to have once rolled around on the ground punching and kicking "the nicest guy in the world."

Kawamura somewhat reluctantly agreed with Suzuki-san that another meeting should be scheduled with the remaining Silver Fox, Takashi Sakai. Sakai was retired and lived alone, reported the tennis club office, but the manager had heard that he still did occasional consulting jobs for his former employers, Mitsubishi Heavy Industries. ("His job must have been to pick up the heavy machines," reported Suzuki-san on hearing this piece of information.)

And a session would have to be scheduled with Manabe's new widow after her arrival in Tokyo. It was the type of interview Kawamura liked least. He planned it last, in fact.

Theodore Bitman was found sitting on a tall stool in a sound stage at the Asahi Television studio in Roppongi. It was 10:30 in the morning, but taping was about to begin for a program to be aired at midnight. Six young women wearing semitransparent, loose-fitting negligees and the briefest of underpants were busily stretching, bending over, and otherwise loosening up. Bitman was intently studying them.

"My part of the show is, ah, slightly different," Bitman explained to Kawamura and Suzuki-san.

"My role tonight is to describe the strange eating habits of Americans in the U.S."

"Are their eating habits strange?" asked Kawamura.

"I don't know, I've lived here since 1963, but anyway that's my role in this whole thing."

Suzuki-san, interested in camera and lighting angles, wandered over to where the six young women were now rehearsing a pillow fight under the director's scrutiny.

"It's come to our attention," said Kawamura, "that you and Manabe-san had a disagreement in the past, and the, ah, bad feelings may have continued to the present."

Bitman turned his back to the rehearsals and faced Kawamura directly.

"It was a business disagreement," said Bitman, "not a personal one. In fact, once we settled that . . . problem . . . Shig and I became somewhat friendly again. As I said to you the other day, he was one of the nicest guys in the world. We are . . . were . . . business rivals, but in a way, I respected him."

"Could you describe the . . . 'business disagreement'?"

Bitman glanced briefly over his shoulder. The six young women now had their negligees off and were rolling around the floor in their underpants while a person dressed up in a panda costume was pretending to nuzzle them with his snout. The director was shouting instructions—the panda kept getting it wrong.

"To be honest," said Bitman turning back to Kawamura, "I'm a little embarrassed about it. I approached Shig in 1964 and asked him to lend me money to start my own business. Shig was already established as a pearl importer-exporter, and I merely wanted to set up a retail store for pearls in Japan. He put up money for the deposit with the landlord and introduced me to pearl suppliers. I still have that first store in the Ginza, by the way."

"Why would someone like Manabe-san lend money for something like that?"

Bitman thought for a moment.

"I don't know for sure," he said. "As I said, he *was* a nice guy, plus I think he appreciated the fact I was a foreigner who bothered to learn Japanese. Actually, I studied Japanese in Salt Lake City and came to Tokyo for my church."

"What was the disagreement?"

"Friends of mine in the States were looking for supplies of pearls . . . and I began supplying them. *That* suddenly was in competition with Shig. He was upset, and wanted repayment on the loan. I think his wife was a factor in the decision."

The six young women, now wearing baby panda outfits that came down to their waists, were rehearsing dance steps with the adult panda. Cameramen were on the floor shooting upward, and the director was still shouting instructions.

"The problem is," continued Bitman, "I had just opened my fourth and fifth retail store, and I didn't have cash."

"And . . . ?"

"And Shig sued me. As I say, I think his wife had a lot to do with that. She is probably stronger in business than he . . . was."

"What happened?"

"We settled. Manabe has owned ten percent of Bitman Pearls since 1967. It's been very good for him . . . them, if I do say so."

"Ten percent is a lot to take off the top of a business," suggested Kawamura.

"Not to me," said Bitman waving his arm around the studio, "I earn more than ten percent of my business doing this crap."

The six young women, now wearing dressing gowns and looking like high school girls, were huddled together eating box lunches from containers with cute little cartoon characters on them as Kawamura and Suzuki-san—the latter somewhat reluctantly—left the studio. Bitman was being seated at a desk, and a microphone was being fitted around his neck.

The lunch-hour crowds were beginning to fill the sidewalks as Kawamura and Suzuki-san got to the Kanda section of Tokyo. Kimura-san, he of the fancy cravat and paisley shirt, worked in the heart of the bookstore district for a Japanese-American publishing company. He was assigned to the company's main bookstore—a narrow building with three floors and a preponderance of books in English.

It took a moment or two to locate Kimura. His job mainly involved checking inventory and keeping the shelves full. In the grand scheme of things, Kimura was not part of the upper hierarchy.

Kimura eventually emerged from a back-room area which, a quick glance through the doors revealed, contained a great number of cardboard boxes. He was wearing a yellowish-white shirt. His worn trousers were sprung at the knees.

"We can't talk here," announced Kimura. "Perhaps some lunch?"

Kawamura and Suzuki-san followed Kimura down a narrow street, up a narrow alley, and into a coffee shop which, because of its limited menu, kept the lunch-hour crowds to a minimum— mainly students and other impoverished individuals.

"You've heard that I used to work for Shig Manabe," announced Kimura as soon as they were seated.

"What we've heard," said Kawamura, "is that you and Manabe-san once had a fight that involved actual blows on the tennis club courts. It seems so unlikely, from what we've heard about the man."

The waitress arrived and took three orders of "pizza toast" and coffee from the men.

"We don't speak . . . *didn't* speak," said Kimura.

"Why?" asked Kawamura.

"Jobs are personal things, they require individual satisfaction. Shig was always so busy being nice, he didn't recognize the needs of people working for him."

"What does that mean?"

"It means he was more concerned about his . . . image . . . than he was about those who did the actual work."

"What was your job?" asked Kawamura.

"It was an important job. I would negotiate the price of pearls in Japan, then travel to New York to provide details, then return to Japan to finish the arrangements. I enjoyed it."

"What went wrong?"

"Airmail, telexes, and eventually fax machines," said Kimura. "Manabe decided, or at least his wife decided, that they didn't need personal contacts anymore."

"What happened?"

The waitress delivered thick slices of lightly toasted bread with tomato paste and cheese spread on top.

"What happened? What happened is that they offered me a job as a supply manager—a Japan-only position."

"But . . . "

"It reduced my status," said Kimura. I would no longer be an international businessman.

"You discussed it with . . . ?"

"*Discussed* it? I told him I was better than a supply manager. Then I hit him. On court number nine."

The three men addressed their pizza toast.

"And I told him I would never talk to him the rest of my life."

"Last Saturday at the club . . . , " began Kawamura.

"I had nothing to do with last Saturday at the club. I said I would never talk to him the rest of *my* life . . . not *his* life."

Kimura took another bite of his pizza toast.

"I already told you," said Kimura looking down at his plate, "Shig Manabe was still a very good man."

Kimura swallowed the pizza toast. He then sat up straight and looked at his watch.

"I'm afraid I must get back to my job," he announced. "I have a responsibility to my employers."

Kimura rose and left the restaurant. Kawamura and Suzuki-san finished the pizza toast, then left the restaurant, Kawamura paying the bill for all of them.

Kawamura and Suzuki-san stood on the crowded sidewalk as Kawamura called the station from a public telephone outside a candy store. The roar of passing traffic made it difficult to hear.

"Sakai," Kawamura shouted into the receiver. "Do we have an appointment with him yet?" Kawamura did not want to go all the way out to Ueno without confirmation that the visit would bear fruit.

The voice on the other end was ignoring Sakai

and was instead saying something about Shig Manabe's wife.

"I know," yelled Kawamura, "we're going there later. I want to know about Sakai."

The voice kept talking about Manabe's wife. Suzuki-san wandered into the candy store.

"A burglary? What's that got to do with us?" Pedestrians were now giving Kawamura a wide berth on the sidewalk.

The burglary issue would not go away. The voice mentioned that it was Chief Arai's urgent request that Kawamura go immediately to the Manabe residence.

"OK," said Kawamura, "but keep trying to get in touch with Sakai."

Kawamura hung up as Suzuki-san wandered out of the candy store. His mouth was full—the pizza toast obviously not having been enough.

"Something happened at Manabe's house. His wife is back from the States, and the chief wants us to go there immediately."

"Subway or taxi?" asked Suzuki-san. "The subway will be faster."

"Taxi," replied Kawamura without hesitation.

The Manabe residence in Tokyo was a penthouse in a high-rise apartment complex know as Hiroo Towers. The Manabes owned the apartment, located behind one of the major shopping and congregating areas for foreigners in Tokyo. It was down the hill from the Tokyo Lawn Tennis Club.

Kawamura and Suzuki-san were buzzed into the building by security machinery and entered the elevator bound for the thirteenth floor. Plush, in a word, described the surroundings.

The door to the Manabe apartment was opened by the very tan man Kawamura first met in jockey shorts, then later in the head-to-toe Nike outfit. His name was Hanada.

"Ahhh," said Kawamura.

"Yes, we've met. Remember I told you I was distantly related to Shig. His father's cousin . . . "

" . . . was married to your grandfather. I remember," said Kawamura. "What happened here?"

"Let me introduce you to Mrs. Manabe first. I'm afraid she's quite upset."

Kawamura took off his shoes and entered the living room of the apartment. The decor was Western, sparse, ultramodern, and looked for all the world like a first-class hotel room. Two uniformed policemen from the Azabu Police Station were standing awkwardly on both sides of the large picture window at the end of the room.

Mrs. Manabe—Shirley Caplan Manabe was her complete name—was seated on a couch with two large suitcases on the floor next to her. She was a large-boned woman with a mass of gray-blond hair, and she was obviously in a state of stress.

"I'm sorry about your husband," said Kawamura after they were introduced.

"He was too soft-hearted," said Mrs. Manabe in English. "And look where it got him."

"Well, er, we're trying to solve the . . . problem."
Kawamura was not perfectly comfortable speaking English.

Shirley Manabe stood up. She was probably a foot taller than Shig Manabe had been.

"And now the disgrace of having our personal possessions searched."

"I've heard that there was some kind of . . . burglary?" Kawamura looked at the two policemen by the window and asked them in Japanese if there had been a burglary. The two policemen shrugged their shoulders slightly.

"They ransacked this place," said Mrs. Manabe, starting to sob.

Kawamura looked around. If anything was out of place, it certainly wasn't obvious.

"Mrs. Manabe is quite sure of it," said Hanada.

"I'm afraid you'll have to show me," said Kawamura.

Shirley Manabe led Kawamura into the one bedroom. It contained a bed larger than anything Kawamura had ever seen before, a bureau, and two small tables on either side of the bed. Other than an ashtray with a few cigarette butts in it, there was no sign anyone had lived there. Clearly, the Manabe household had been established in the United States.

"I'm slowly adjusting to my husband's death," said Mrs. Manabe opening the top drawer of the bureau, "but I can't adjust to this."

Kawamura looked at the jumble of women's underwear in the drawer.

"And look at this," said Mrs. Manabe opening the second drawer.

Kawamura looked at the jumble of men's underwear in the second drawer.

"And this."

Kawamura looked at the clothes hanging neatly on hangers in the closet Mrs. Manabe had just opened.

"It's as if the final insult to the man was to violate our private lives," stated Mrs. Manabe.

"I'm not really certain I see . . . "

"Then look at this," said Mrs. Manabe striding back into the living room. She walked over to a small desk next to the window. She opened the top drawer. Inside were various piles of paper—some face-up, some face-down—but to Kawamura nothing seemed particularly out of the ordinary.

"This is a mess," said Mrs. Manabe starting to sob again.

Kawamura turned to the two policemen still standing by the window. "Are there signs of breaking and entering?" he asked in Japanese. They offered more shrugs and little twitches indicating that there were not.

"I have asked our men," said Kawamura to Mrs. Manabe, "to make a thorough investigation. But . . . when you feel up to it . . . you will have to make a list of anything that is missing."

Mrs. Manabe had returned to the couch, but her face was buried in her handkerchief. Further conversation was impossible. Kawamura signaled Suzuki-san, who was wandering around in the background, and went toward the front door. Hanada accompanied them to the entrance hallway.

"I guess . . . you'll have to keep an eye on her," said Kawamura.

"I will do that," said Hanada. "After all, we're . . . "

" . . . distantly related. I remember."

Kawamura and Suzuki-san were bowed out of the apartment, but after the door shut Suzuki-san put his hand on Kawamura's arm. He indicated the lock on the door.

Kawamura bent over and looked at it carefully. The hallway light was not very bright, but it was possible to see two shiny spots on either side of the keyhole in the brass lock.

"Professional?"

"Could be," answered Suzuki-san.

"We'd better send someone over from the station to help those two patrolmen."

Kawamura straightened and began to walk along the hallway to the elevator.

"There was another interesting thing," said Suzuki-san.

He opened his hand. Inside, cradled in his palm, was a cigarette butt. It clearly bore traces of lipstick.

"And Mrs. Manabe wasn't smoking," he observed.

CHAPTER 14

The Tuesday morning meeting in Chief Arai's office involved the same dynamic questioning and words of wisdom as the day before.

"You idiots have nothing to show for all your work," observed the chief. "Do I have to go out there and do every damn thing myself?"

For some reason the newspapers and television people had not been headlining the story of the death at the tennis club. The chances were that former Ambassador Morimoto, now the club president, had called in favors and was otherwise exercising influence. This calmed Chief Arai only slightly.

"Look, you fools, I want *answers,* not theories. If you can't come up with an answer in twenty-four hours, then I want you to pull in some of your fancy suspects and begin official interrogation."

"We value your guidance," said Kawamura rising. "Suzuki-san and I will get busy right away."

Seated at his desk on the third floor, Kawamura looked at Suzuki-san.

"You mean you stayed up last night and watched the show?"

"It ended at one o'clock this morning," answered a yawning Suzuki.

"Our friend Bitman?"

"He talked a lot. As always." Suzuki-san yawned again. "And it's interesting, those girls look . . . bigger . . . on television."

"Well, that certainly is interesting," agreed Kawamura, "but we've got work to do."

Kawamura and Suzuki-san looked at each other.

"We should go to the wake for Manabe-san tonight," said Suzuki-san. "Maybe question some more people."

"You're right," agreed Kawamura. "But that's tonight."

Kawamura and Suzuki-san looked at each other.

"We could go over to the tennis club and measure something. The bath, maybe," suggested Suzuki-san.

"Maybe."

"The lab report regarding the lipstick on the cigarette butt from Manabe's apartment will be here in about an hour," offered Suzuki-san.

"Good."

Kawamura and Suzuki-san looked at each other.

"We still don't have any information on Sakai's whereabouts," said Suzuki-san.

"I know."

Kawamura and Suzuki-san looked at each other.

"Our experts can't prove that someone broke into Manabe's apartment, but if it was done professionally, it would be hard to prove," said Suzuki-san.

"Has she come up with a list of things stolen?"

"No. She told our people that nothing was missing, but that someone had definitely searched the place," said Suzuki-san. "I can understand that. If someone looked through my place, I'd know."

"It was probably one of Manabe-san's girl-friends. By the way, what the Frenchman said was 'Look for the woman'."

Kawamura and Suzuki-san looked at each other.

"I could go over to the club and see if I can get the staff to tell me more about Manabe's . . . friends," suggested Suzuki-san.

"And I could go out and stop strangers on the street and ask them."

Kawamura and Suzuki-san looked at each other. Then Suzuki-san looked up at the ceiling in the general direction of Chief Arai's office.

"We'd better do *something*," said Suzuki-san, "before . . . "

"You're right," said Kawamura rising from his chair. "Let's go over to the club."

But the telephone suddenly ringing on Kawamura's desk brought a message which changed the course of everything.

CHAPTER 15

"It's the heat. They probably wouldn't have noticed during the rest of the year."

Kawamura and Suzuki-san were on the subway to Ueno. It was faster than a car, and Kawamura would put up with the steps.

"I've told them not to touch anything," continued Kawamura, "but it's not our jurisdiction and . . . they're interested in removing the body . . . the heat . . . "

"Remember the body you found in the sauna at the American Club?" asked Suzuki-san. "It was probably just as bad . . . "

Kawamura nudged Suzuki-san in the ribs. Fellow passengers in the subway were tuning into the conversation and beginning to step away.

Kawamura, puffing, and Suzuki-san emerged from the subway and walked across the street to a small police box on the corner.

The young patrolman knew exactly where the building was—back across the street next to the subway entrance.

"You got here just in time," said the Ueno police captain who greeted Kawamura. They were standing in the entranceway to Sakai's small apartment. "The heat . . . "

"I understand," said Kawamura, "and I appreciate it." Indeed, the entire building seemed to be filled with the stench of death.

Kawamura walked into the room. The smell was even worse. Several uniformed policemen, cloth masks over their noses and mouths, were carefully lifting Sakai, loosening the belt around his neck, and then laying him gently on the floor of the kitchenette. The process took about a minute.

"One of the neighbors complained about the smell," explained the Ueno captain. "We forced open the door. It was locked. That chair was tipped over on the floor."

"Where are his glasses?" asked Kawamura. The bloated face of the Silver Fox gazed upward.

"Over here," said a young man in plain clothes.

The glasses, one thick lens broken, lay on the floor in the middle of the living-dining-sleeping room.

"Did anyone move them?" asked Kawamura.

"No sir," said the young plainclothes man.

"Can we remove the body now?" asked the Ueno captain. Police ambulance personnel were hovering in the doorway.

"Yes, thank you," said Kawamura. "But could you arrange for a complete autopsy?"

"Of course," said the Ueno captain.

"How did you think of calling the Azabu station?" Kawamura asked.

"Look around. Wrongful-death information at

your tennis club was already circulated to all the stations. And yet nothing was really reported in the press."

Kawamura looked around. Here was a place where a person had lived. Clothing was all over, dishes and glasses were piled on top of the television set, and newspapers and magazines were strewn about the floor. Clearly, no woman had ever set foot in the apartment.

But aside from a few purely personal touches—a couple of photographs of Sakai with a woman, probably his wife, a photograph of Sakai as a young boy with obvious parents, and Sakai in a school graduation photo—everything else was the Tokyo Lawn Tennis Club.

There were Sakai and Manabe in a photograph standing in front of the old clubhouse—a dilapidated structure that was something of an eyesore in the ritzy Azabu neighborhood—accepting a trophy. He and Manabe were not Silver Foxes then, they were black-haired, well-fit club champions. Manabe's arm was around Sakai's shoulders.

Another photograph, obviously taken a few years later, showed Sakai and Manabe clowning around with a racket that appeared to have a ribbon attached to it. Sakai was bowing low as he handed the racket to Manabe.

Yet another photograph showed Sakai and Manabe sitting next to each other in tuxedos at a formal party. On one side sat the woman who must have been Sakai's wife, and on the other,

Shirley Manabe, looking younger, and bigger. A Tokyo Lawn Tennis Club banner loomed in the background.

A fourth photograph, framed and in a position of honor on the middle shelf of a bookcase, showed Sakai and Manabe, looking haggard and exhausted but not quite at the Silver Fox stage, standing next to the Japanese Crown Prince—and now current Emperor of Japan—and a younger Tatsuo Morimoto, former ambassador and current club president.

On the floor next to the front door was an athletic bag with a Tokyo Lawn Tennis Club ninetieth-anniversary green-and-white medallion attached. The clothing in the bag was clean and ready to go.

"I see," said Kawamura. "Again, thank you for notifying us. "

Kawamura and the Ueno captain walked toward the entrance. The police ambulance people had already left with their deteriorating cargo. Ueno policemen were crowding into the room and beginning the measuring and photographing routine. Suzuki-san stood in the doorway. He was surrounded by a new group—this time, of newspaper reporters.

"Is it true," asked members of the press in one form or another, "that the murder at the Tokyo Lawn Tennis Club is solved?"

"I have no idea what you're talking about," answered Suzuki-san immediately, staring at Kawamura.

CHAPTER 16

Shig Manabe's wake was appropriate for one of the nicest guys in the world. Held at the Aoyama cemetery facility, several kilometers from the tennis club, the attendees included a broad mixture of people who had come in contact with Manabe down through the years.

Black-suited businessmen somberly paid their respects. Black-dressed women wept silently but genuinely. Members of the Tokyo Lawn Tennis Club were the predominant group. All in all, nearly a thousand people paid their respects to this remarkable man.

Kawamura and Suzuki-san recognized Nat Forrest, Discoverer of the Body. He was one of the genuinely grieved. Kimura-san, former employee and now in charge of bookstore inventory, was resplendent in a black suit and tie. The Frenchman was sobbing uncontrollably. Various club employees, including the office manager, the court manager, members of the office staff, and one of the tennis club waitresses, hovered in the background. The man Kawamura first met in a blue blazer, polka-dot tie, and underpants, was there wearing his blue blazer and polka-dot tie. He kept looking at his Rolex watch. Kawamura had to force the image of the man's underpants out of his mind.

Theodore Bitman was there and spent most of the time in the back of the room chatting with photographers.

Shirley Manabe, the brand-new widow, was escorted by her distant relative Hanada-san and the club's president, former Ambassador Morimoto. Mrs. Manabe looked devastated, and a gray-haired man Kawamura did not recognize walked up and put an arm around her.

Given the circumstances of his death, Manabe-san's coffin was closed. People nevertheless knelt or bowed in front of the macabre missile. Kawamura decided there and then to have his body cremated and spread across the Pacific before anyone noticed he was gone.

Suzuki-san had wandered off in the direction of the waitress as Kawamura sat in a folding chair and ate cake.

"It's a terrible thing," said a voice at Kawamura's elbow. "But at least the mystery is solved."

Kawamura looked at the man who had seated himself in the next chair.

"The mystery? I'm not sure *any* mystery has been solved."

"The papers were very flattering about your detection abilities. Finding Sakai's body."

Morimoto, club president, was calmly eating a piece of cake.

"It's still only an *apparent* suicide, and we're not certain *why* he . . . "

"No one is certain why anybody does anything. It's a normal characteristic of human nature."

"But they were friends . . . "

"Friends," said the former ambassador, "kill each other more than strangers kill each other."

Morimoto went off to greet people. Kawamura finished his cake—there'd be no food left by the time he made it home—then got up with the intention of finding Suzuki-san.

Hanada approached.

"There you are. You can't imagine how relieved I am."

"About what?" asked Kawamura.

Hanada took Kawamura by the arm and led him toward the door to the room.

"I know it, and I think you knew it," said Hanada cryptically.

"I know many things, but . . . "

"She's basically a good woman."

Hanada indicated by a nod of his head a woman standing talking to three men in the corner. Kawamura had noticed her before. Tall, and possessed of a figure more substantial than the average Japanese, she had attracted considerable attention even in her black dress and veil. She was a good dozen years younger than Hanada.

"My wife," amplified Hanada. "She had been having an affair with Shig Manabe for years. And until we found out about Sakai, I was afraid you suspected me."

Hanada flicked a crumb off the lapel of his black suit.

"You know," said Hanada, "Shig and I . . . "

" . . . were distant relatives," confirmed Kawamura.

"That was the problem," said Hanada shrugging his shoulders, then hurrying off to join his wife and the three men in the corner.

Kawamura and Suzuki-san met up in the entranceway just outside the room containing Shig Manabe's corpse.

"You won't believe what I just learned," announced Suzuki-san.

The two men walked down the graveled walk to the main street running past the Aoyama cemetery. Taxis, if they were lucky, would be waiting.

"The waitress from the club," said Suzuki-san, "admitted to . . . 'being close' . . . to Manabe."

"Being close? What does that mean?"

"They, you know, *did* it."

"Did it?"

"Yes, did it. She visited him in his apartment," said Suzuki-san.

"When?"

"When? Seventeen times in the last six months."

Taxis whizzed past, not even slowing and teasing.

"But what's more interesting," continued Suzuki-san, "is that the waitress just got engaged to be married."

"Good for her," pronounced Kawamura.

"Good for her is right. Her fiancé is the D.O.B."

More taxis whizzed past.

"D.O.B.? What the hell is that?"

"You taught me that," said Suzuki-san. "Discoverer of the Body. Nat Forrest."

Taxis were not stopping. Kawamura and Suzuki-san decided to walk across the street to Chez Pierre's—a French café.

"And even *more* interesting," said Suzuki-san as the two men were being seated at a tiny table near the window, "is that Nat Forrest works for Mr. Hanada—your friend who . . . "

" . . . is distantly related to Shig Manabe," confirmed Kawamura.

The waiter, speaking pretend-French, took their order.

"Merde," said Kawamura, in keeping with the spirit and atmosphere of his thoughts.

CHAPTER 17

The Wednesday morning meeting in Chief Arai's office brought things to a head.

"The Golden Bear partner of Manabe . . . "

"Silver Fox," corrected Kawamura.

" . . . Silver Fox partner of Manabe killed him, and then killed himself," expounded Arai.

"Come on," said Kawamura, "we don't know

that. All we know is that Sakai is dead. I think there's a . . . "

"But it's a solution, or at least a plausible solution, to everything that happened."

"But I think that . . . "

"You think what?" bellowed Arai. "I pay you for solutions, not for thinking. The case is now off the books."

"There are indications . . . "

"Indications? Don't use that fancy talk with me. Do you have any solid evidence that Sakai did *not* kill Manabe?"

Kawamura glanced briefly at Suzuki-san.

"No, we do not have solid evidence, but after interviewing everybody . . . "

"Interviewing? A solution falls into your lap, and you're still concerned about . . . what?"

"I'm concerned about a killer getting away from us. From the police," said Kawamura.

Chief Arai looked down at the notes on his desk.

"Lipstick, affairs with distant relatives, waitresses who are compromised, former employees, former business partners, mysterious searches of apartments, a kid working for a relative—it's all a jumble."

"That's the point," said Kawamura. "It's still a jumble."

"Whose fault is that?" roared Arai.

"My feeling, Chief Arai, is that Sakai could not and did not kill Manabe-san. There's more involved than that. And I don't think he took his own life." Kawamura paused for a moment. "It's my feeling."

Arai turned and looked out the window at the Roppongi morning traffic.

"You know what I think about 'feelings' entering detective work, Captain Kawamura?"

"Ah, yes sir, we've discussed it before."

Chief Arai continued looking out the window.

"Confessions and convictions are the twin jewels of our success," he added.

"Ah, yes sir, we've discussed it before."

"But you still 'feel' something is wrong about this tennis club thing?"

"Yes sir, I do."

A minute passed. Kawamura stared at the back of Chief Arai's head. Suzuki-san rubbed his eyes, then looked at the floor.

"The press is satisfied with the results," said Chief Arai.

"I know that."

Chief Arai belched.

"How much longer?" he asked.

"I don't know. A few days."

"OK," said Arai. "But Kawamura-kun . . . "

"Yes sir?"

"Be careful."

"Yes sir."

Kawamura and Suzuki-san left the chief's office. Arai was still looking out the window.

Down on the third floor Kawamura and Suzuki-san discussed alternatives.

"I want to spend more time with Mrs. Manabe
. . . preferably without her distant relative Hanada
around."

"The funeral is this morning and . . . "

"We're not going," said Kawamura. "See if you
can find out when she'll be back to her apartment."

Suzuki-san wandered off.

Kawamura picked up the phone and put a call
through to his new friend at the Ueno Police
Station. The information he obtained was interesting—Sakai indeed died as a result of the hanging, but he had also suffered intermediate
hemorrhaging in the stomach immediately prior
to his death.

"Maybe he got hit by a ball," suggested the
captain from Ueno.

"He was a tennis player," responded Kawamura,
"not a bowler."

"Good point," said the Ueno connection. "And
one more thing. The glasses you asked about.
They were shatterproof plastic."

"Because of tennis," Kawamura observed. "How
could they be broken?"

"Someone stepped on them wearing shoes,"
answered the man in Ueno. "And from what we
can tell, it was a 'shoes-off' house. Sakai wasn't
wearing any."

"Keep a second copy of your report on ice,"
suggested Kawamura.

"In the trunk of my wife's car," said the Ueno

captain. "It looks like your problem and our problem are related."

"It looks that way," agreed Kawamura.

A clerk approached Kawamura as he hung up the phone.

"Here is the report you asked for," said the clerk. "It confirms the details of Manabe-san's lawsuit against Mr. Bitman."

"Any surprises?"

"No sir," said the clerk. "As your interview report indicated, Mr. Bitman settled it by ceding ten percent of his business to Manabe-san."

The clerk started to walk away. He was a young man, very intense, and like his counterparts everywhere in Japan, virtually invaluable.

"Wait a minute," said Kawamura. "Use your network again and see if you can find out how the newspapers found out so quickly about Sakai's death in Ueno and the connection with the tennis club here in Azabu."

"No problem, sir," said the clerk as he walked away.

Suzuki-san returned with the news that the funeral was scheduled to begin in an hour, cremation would be immediately afterwards, and Mrs. Manabe planned to return to her apartment to rest at about 2:30.

"It must be difficult for her to go through all this, and still be jet-lagged," observed Suzuki-san.

"You're probably right," said Kawamura, "but we'll have to talk to her as soon as possible. I think we have to learn more about Manabe-san.

He apparently was a nice man, but something . . ."

"You don't plan to tell her about . . . the women? That would just be another shock for . . ."

"Don't worry, my friend," said Kawamura standing, "we want her to tell *us* things. Come on, we're going to pay another visit to the tennis club."

CHAPTER 18

"The place looks deserted," said Suzuki-san as they entered the club lobby.

"It's a weekday, and the funeral's today."

The lady at the reception desk stood as Kawamura and Suzuki-san approached the wooden doors to the clubhouse.

"Good morning," said Kawamura pleasantly.

"Good morning," said the lady. No doubt about it, she was blushing slightly.

"I would imagine things are rather slow today."

"Well, the manager is attending the, ah, funeral, but people are here."

Kawamura looked at the sign-in book. There were quite a few signatures in it.

"It's not that surprising," said the lady, as if reading Kawamura's thoughts. Many of the weekday players, particularly the newer members, didn't know Manabe-san."

Kawamura and Suzuki-san walked through the wooden doors, and sure enough there were forty or fifty people either playing tennis or relaxing in the clubhouse. Most were women, but there were perhaps a dozen men. One of them was the Frenchman.

"Bonjour, mon capitaine."

"Er, yes," said Kawamura. "Good morning. You're not at the funeral?"

The Frenchman suddenly looked very sad.

"It so sad a thing," he said. Kawamura thought for a moment the man would break into tears again. "I was at the ceremony last night . . . "

"I noticed," said Kawamura. Suzuki-san wandered off. "And I also noticed," continued Kawamura, "that people seemed relieved that . . . the mystery is solved."

The Frenchman's expression did not change. He took Kawamura by the arm.

"I have the business client coming here soon," said the Frenchman, "but could we talk briefly?"

The Frenchman led Kawamura to a table and chairs—coincidentally the same ones Kawamura and Morimoto had occupied earlier.

"Can I get for you the coffee?"

"No, thank you," said Kawamura.

"Two coffee," signaled the Frenchman with a flourish. "But first, I should introduce myself. I am Jean-Pierre Toulon."

Business cards were exchanged. Kawamura asked if he could write on Toulon's card."

"But of course."

Monsieur Toulon became "Too Long" in Kawamura's phonetic method for remembering the names of foreigners.

"The thing I wish to say," said Toulon softly, "is that Manabe for one reason or another was the very respected man in this club."

"That's what I understand."

"And for one reason or another Sakai was not the popular man in this club."

Toulon sat back and shrugged his shoulders.

"Don't you think that the . . . symmetry is too obvious?" asked Toulon. "I mean, in life, there never is such a balance."

The waitress delivered two coffees.

"You must have the coffee," Toulon urged. "It is morning."

"Why was Sakai so unpopular?" asked Kawamura after the waitress, whom he had never seen before, left the table.

"Very simple. He did not want to be popular," answered Toulon. "To him, the idea of this club was a place to play tennis with his friend Manabe. He was not interested in the social activity." The Frenchman shrugged. "Many people are like that, *n'est-ce pas?*"

"Did you ever play tennis with him?"

"No. Never," answered Toulon. "Why would he like to play tennis with *me?* I was not his friend, and he did not want me for his friend."

"How do you know . . . ?"

"I should explain. I have a small restaurant. The food is only fair—some bread, some *fromage,* a very good crepe, on some days there is excellent fish, baked . . . "

"I understand," interrupted Kawamura.

" . . . but the wine is outstanding, plus liqueurs of all kinds, and of course . . . "

"I understand, but how do you know . . . "

"Of course, forgive me," begged the Frenchman. "On many occasions when he is in Tokyo, mostly the weekend time, Manabe comes to my small place. And always with Sakai."

"Did they argue?"

"No. Never. They were friends. They ate. They drank. They talked about the old days. They laughed. They even cried. They were friends."

Toulon shrugged his shoulders.

"And that's why I say," he continued, "it is not true, this symmetry. The worst man kills the best man. Never. I believe with all my heart that Sakai killed himself *because* he lost his best friend."

"You understand what that means, of course?"

"Naturally. The killer is still with us," said Toulon matter-of-factly.

The Frenchman rose from his chair.

"Excuse, please," he said, still looking sad, "the client has arrived for the game."

Kawamura finished his coffee and went looking for Suzuki-san.

He found him at the far end of the courts, in a slightly separate area obviously used for practice. A green board with a horizontal line the height of a tennis net painted on it loomed at one end.

Suzuki-san was with the court manager and what turned out to be the head groundsman. The court manager was furtively smoking a cigarette, and both club employees were periodically glancing back at the clubhouse.

"You found us," said Suzuki-san, stating the obvious.

"Yes," said Kawamura. "And we want to thank you gentlemen for all the help you've given us. It's been a . . . sad time."

The club employees accepted the gracious comment with nods.

"We are still very concerned about the developments here," continued Kawamura. "And any additional information you can give us is appreciated."

Kawamura picked up two tennis balls lying on the cement surface.

"Are you a tennis player, Captain?" asked the court manager.

"No, baseball."

Kawamura turned and fired a tennis ball at the green board. It hit exactly at the "T" formed by the painted net and the painted center line. He threw the second ball, and it hit at exactly the same spot.

"Two more?" asked the head groundsman.

"A thousand yen?" asked Kawamura.

"You're on," said the head groundsman.

Kawamura picked up two more balls, whapped them against the wall in the identical spot, took the thousand yen note from the head groundsman, and put it in his pocket.

The subsequent meeting, which lasted about ten minutes, revealed that Shig Manabe may have been the nicest guy in the world, but he had the alarming habit of treating those he considered to be his inferiors with a cavalier attitude that bordered on rudeness. In fact, it was somewhat surprising that Sakai would be friends with Manabe. Sakai did not "kiss the ass" of fellow members, but he was a "real person" with the staff. Sakai and Manabe may have "fought like Europeans" with each other during tennis, but Sakai wouldn't harm a fly.

The meeting over, Kawamura picked up two more balls.

"Double or nothing?"

"Why not?" responded the head groundsman.

Kawamura fired the first ball and it hit the exact spot in the "T." The second ball was high and wide to the right. Kawamura took two thousand yen from his wallet and handed it to the head groundsman.

"I'm getting old," he said.

CHAPTER 19

Kawamura and Suzuki-san stood in the plush lobby of Hiroo Towers waiting for the elevator. It was slightly before 2:30.

"We could always use the stairway and walk up," suggested Suzuki-san.

Kawamura looked at his sweating assistant.

"Thirteen floors is no problem for me," said Kawamura, "but I think we should wait."

The elevator finally arrived, Kawamura and Suzuki-san stepped in, and the doors were just closing as Shirley Manabe, dressed in black, entered.

"I am very tired," said Mrs. Manabe.

"We know that," said Kawamura, "and we'll be as quick as we can. But there are things we must know about your late husband before you leave."

"All there is to know about my husband is that he is dead," said Mrs. Manabe looking up at the floor-indicator in the elevator.

"I understand. We're just trying to find out why."

Mrs. Manabe said nothing, the doors opened,

and the policemen followed her down the corridor to her apartment.

"I have friends calling for me at 6:00," she said, "and I *would* like to take a nap before that."

Mrs. Manabe unlocked the apartment door—the two shiny dots next to the keyhole were now as bright as lighthouse beacons to Kawamura. Under protest from the men, Mrs. Manabe made tea.

Finally, seated in the living room, Mrs. Manabe began to talk.

"My life with Shig began when we met at the University of Michigan. All I knew about his past is what he told me. It wasn't much. I like to think that's when . . . his life began."

Mrs. Manabe was dangerously close to tears.

"He was a remarkable man," offered Kawamura.

"He was a remarkable man, and he was a simple man. The pearl business was actually started by my father. I had to watch Shig. If we weren't careful, he would have given the business away to his friends."

Suzuki-san, not wandering, was seated on the couch and nodding sympathetically. Kawamura knew Suzuki-san understood between five and seven words in English.

"For many years, I did the day-to-day work, and Shig maintained the contacts," said Mrs. Manabe.

"One of his friends, of course, was Sakai. Was he ever in business with . . . ?"

"Sakai? He built factories. And power plants. I don't think he ever *saw* a pearl."

"You know that Sakai is thought to have . . . been involved in Shi . . . your husband's death?"

"It was in the papers," said Mrs. Manabe. "To be honest, I don't care. Nothing will bring Shig back.

Mrs. Manabe leaned her head against the back of the chair.

"Did you know Sakai very well?"

"Not really. He didn't particularly . . . 'approve' of me."

"Why?" asked Kawamura.

"I was an American. He was the type of old-fashioned person who couldn't deal with Japan being 'humiliated' by America in the war."

"Do you think he could have actually . . . ah, murdered your husband?"

Mrs. Manabe sat up and took a sip of tea.

"I told you," she said, "I don't care. I'm going to pack up and get out of here."

"But it's important to us," said Kawamura. "For example, I don't think he could have . . . murdered your husband."

Mrs. Manabe leaned her head against the back of the chair again.

"Sakai was Shig's oldest friend. He was a big baby, but he would never hurt my husband."

Suzuki-san nodded sympathetically. Kawamura was afraid Mrs. Manabe would fall asleep.

"What I *do* think is that somebody broke into this apartment looking for something of Shig's," said Kawamura.

"So do I," said Mrs. Manabe after a moment. "It's a relief to hear that somebody believes me."

"What could that be? Did he conduct business out of here, or anything?"

"No," said Mrs. Manabe drowsily. "All business was managed from New York. His personal things were done in his 'hole'."

"His hole?"

"That's what he called it. His hole. And they'd never find that."

"Wait a minute. His hole? Personal things? What's that all about?"

Mrs. Manabe paused for a moment before answering. She *was* falling asleep.

"His hole is where he wrote things," said Mrs. Manabe.

"*What* things?"

"He would never let me in there."

"What . . . ?"

"It's where he was writing the story of his life. His memoirs, he called it."

CHAPTER 20

It had taken a good fifteen minutes to convince Shirley Manabe to get up from the couch, put her shoes on, and lead Kawamura and Suzuki-san to the hole. Kawamura used all the arguments and techniques he could think of—"reaching the ultimate truth," "for the good of humanity," "to prevent defamation of character," and "to preserve integrity." She finally agreed to lead them on the ten-minute walk to the hole.

"The only time I was here was on the day he rented the place," said Mrs. Manabe. They were crossing the Tengenji intersection and moving from the high-rent district to an area still abounding with small shops, stores, and houses.

"Do you have a key for this place?" asked Kawamura.

"'Keys are dangerous' is what Shig always used to say."

The trio plunged into a maze of narrow streets.

"I will have to arrange to have all this stuff packed up and sent back to New York," said Mrs. Manabe.

Kawamura sincerely hoped "this stuff" would not include whips, chains, photographs of naked waitresses or distant relatives, and God knows what else.

"He was very secretive. And he used to say that he could do the research better in Japan."

The group was now in a small shopping area. Merchants' wares overflowed their small stores and onto the sidewalk. Housewives walked back and forth with shopping bags buying fruits and vegetables.

Mrs. Manabe paused at a corner.

"It's either here, or . . . "

Mrs. Manabe stared down a narrow side street. A fish vendor tried to interest Kawamura in a cod.

"No, it's the next corner," said Mrs. Manabe.

"Remember, it's been three or four years since I've been here."

The group reached the next corner, and it was the correct one. At the end of a narrow street was a yakitori restaurant. Mrs. Manabe strode purposefully toward it.

"You don't think," said Suzuki-san softly to Kawamura and looking very concerned, "that this place is a . . . love nest?

"I hope not," answered Kawamura. "But we have no choice."

Mrs. Manabe walked into the yakitori restaurant. The proprietor was, coincidentally, named Suzuki.

There was a moment or two of confusion, but eventually Suzuki the restaurateur came to grips with things.

"Ah," he said in his limited English, "Manabe-san, I have not recognize you. I am . . . sorry . . . about your . . . man. He was the best in the world."

Kawamura introduced himself and Suzuki-san. Suzuki and Suzuki-san made no comments about their names.

"He would come here almost every day," explained Suzuki. "He would work for several hours, come down and have lunch with us, then go back up to work. It was very pleasant."

"Has anyone been here since he . . . died?" asked Kawamura.

"No one has ever been here. You are the first. Even I don't go in there."

Suzuki reached below the yakitori counter and

pulled out a key attached to the end of a small wooden paddle.

Suzuki led the way up a narrow flight of steps opening off a tatami room at the rear of the restaurant.

"We don't use the room since we built our new house," he explained.

At the top of the stairs was a very small landing and one door on the right.

"This is the only key," said Suzuki as he bent down and fitted it into the lock. "He used to say 'keys are dangerous'."

The door opened outward, which meant Mrs. Manabe and Suzuki-san had to step back off the landing and onto the stairs.

Kawamura made a point of entering the room first. It was small, perhaps three meters by two meters. There was one small window opposite the door, but all other wall space was covered floor to ceiling with books and documents on shelves. Filing cabinets stood on either side of the small table in the center of the room. There were at least a dozen piles of neatly stacked documents and albums on the floor.

At the center of the table was a modern computer keyboard, printer, and screen. Next to the word processor on the table was the only framed photograph in the room. It was a picture of Manabe-san in his midteens receiving an award of some kind. He was bowing slightly. All the people in the background, smiling and obviously applauding, were foreigners.

Next to the framed picture was a wooden tray. Inside the tray was a pile of typed pages ten centimeters high. Kawamura looked at the top sheet. It was the conclusion of the manuscript—Shig Manabe's life story.

Mrs. Manabe moved into the room. Kawamura had to step aside as there was really no space to move around. The two Suzukis stood in the doorway looking in.

"Oh my God," was her immediate comment. "I had no *idea* his project was so . . . organized. I thought he just . . . "

Mrs. Manabe began to cry. Kawamura started to put his hand on her shoulder, but decided against it. He looked around the room in an attempt to take in everything he could from where he was standing.

Reference books were in both Japanese and English. Some of the books, particularly the Japanese ones, appeared to be quite old. In a corner of the room, in the small space between the end of a bookcase and the wall, a number of rolled maps or charts leaned at an angle. A small flag on a little wooden stand was on top of one bookcase. The flag was the old Japanese one existing until the end of the Pacific War—the Rising Sun with rays extending to the edge. Nothing in the room, as far as Kawamura could see, had anything to do with pearls.

"I must get out of here," said Mrs. Manabe. "This is all too much for me."

Her sobs shuddered her large frame, and

Kawamura worried about an outburst of hysteria. Kawamura backed out of the room with Mrs. Manabe and stood on the small landing as the two Suzukis entered the room.

"I think it's very important that we examine some of that material." Kawamura was attempting to be both gentle and firm, a task difficult in any case but particularly in a foreign language.

"No," said Mrs. Manabe. "I don't want *anyone* touching Shig's work."

"But there may be something there . . . his manuscript . . . that will help us solve . . . "

"No!" said Mrs. Manabe, this time yelling too loud for the small space. Suzuki the restaurateur emerged from the room looking worried.

"We may be forced to study this so that . . . "

"It's *my* life in there too. And reading about it won't bring Shig back. I *buried* him today."

Mrs. Manabe was understandably close to the edge. Kawamura nodded at the owner of the building and began to lead Mrs. Manabe down the stairs. Suzuki waited until Suzuki-san left the room, then shut and carefully locked the door.

Downstairs, Kawamura watched Suzuki put the key behind the counter.

"We may get a court order to . . . "

"I understand. But in the meantime, *nobody* gets into that room until my friend Manabe-san's wife says so. That's why he trusted me," added the restaurateur.

Kawamura and Suzuki-san dropped Mrs. Manabe off at her apartment, then continued by taxi back to the Azabu Police Station. No one spoke during the trip.

CHAPTER 21

It had happened to Kawamura occasionally in the past—the feeling of being in trouble, the feeling that everyone else knew it, but he wouldn't know why he was in trouble.

Maybe it was the way people looked at him. Or didn't look at him. Sound levels in a room would drop when he'd enter.

Whatever it was, Kawamura had that distinct feeling as he walked toward his desk on the third floor. No one said anything, but a large note was attached to the top of his phone by masking tape. It was an invitation to visit Chief Arai.

Kawamura went upstairs, knocked on Arai's door, and entered. There really were better ways to earn a living.

Kawamura was surprised by his reception, however. The Chief had turned his chair around and was looking out the window—the same position he was in when Kawamura had left the office early that morning.

"Kawamura?" asked Arai without turning around.

"Yes sir."

"Sit down."

Kawamura was already seated.

"Yes sir," he said.

"Do you think there are times when I yell at you too much?" asked Arai.

"Uh, er, not . . . at all," replied Kawamura glibly.

"You realize my . . . advice . . . is for your own good."

"Always, sir. I appreciate it."

Kawamura could hear the sound of the evening rush-hour traffic in Roppongi outside the windows.

"You're a good policeman, Kawamura-kun."

"Oh, not *that* . . . good. Probably because you . . ."

"And I don't often . . . say that kind of thing."

"I know, I mean, I know you can't say that kind of thing . . . your position . . . "

"The murder at the Tokyo Lawn Tennis Club case is closed," interrupted Arai. "And that's official."

Arai turned around and faced Kawamura. The face Kawamura expected to see—bold and blustery—was not there. Instead, the face was gray and pinched.

"But . . . "

"Where are you from?" asked Arai.

"Ah, Kyushu, but . . . "

"What would you be doing if you were not a policeman?"

"Fishing," said Kawamura immediately. "But probably starving," he added.

"As you know, I'm from the other end of Japan . . . Hokkaido."

"I know that, sir." Rumors persisted around the force that Chief Arai was part Russian—on his mother's side.

"And if I were not a policeman, I'd be fishing in Hokkaido. And probably starving," Arai added.

"But . . . "

"Kawamura-kun, the case is closed."

A siren wailed away on the expressway outside the office. Something thumped on the floor above.

"The Ueno Police Station has evidence that Sakai's 'suicide' was not exactly . . . "

"No, they don't," said Chief Arai.

"Yes, they . . . "

"No, they *don't*. I spoke to my counterpart, the chief of that station." Arai paused for a moment. "He . . . received . . . the same instructions."

"The same instructions?"

"The same instructions. Some things, Kawamura-kun, are bigger than us individuals. It's the Japanese way."

"But the truth . . . "

Kawamura stopped. The pain apparent in Arai's eyes was something he had not expected to see.

"I know . . . the 'truth.' It bothers me more than you can ever know," said the peasant from Hokkaido. "It's all we have."

The vehicle with the wailing siren stopped immediately outside Chief Arai's window. The siren did not stop.

"Auto accident," he said.

"Auto accident," Kawamura repeated.

Arai looked down at his hands.

"You have some time off coming, don't you?"

"Three or four days. I've been on duty the last two weekends in a row," said Kawamura.

"You understand that I have to officially report that you will be taking vacation days?"

"I understand that, sir," said Kawamura.

"And I cannot officially take responsibility if there are . . . problems?"

"Yes sir."

Arai looked up from his hands.

"Call me . . . at home . . . to keep me up-to-date."

"Yes sir."

"And Kawamura-kun."

"Yes sir?"

"I just want the truth. I'll take care of the rest."

"Yes sir."

CHAPTER 22

"I heard that the case is closed," said Suzuki-san as Kawamura returned to the third floor. People still seemed to be looking at Kawamura.

"That's the official word," said Kawamura. "I'll be taking the next three or four days off."

"Are we done for the day?" asked Suzuki-san.

"I'm done for the next three or four days."

"Let's have a beer," suggested Suzuki-san.

Kawamura kept his surprise to himself. Although he and Suzuki-san had consumed several thousand liters of beer together, it was never at Suzuki-san's suggestion.

"It's a deal, my friend," replied Kawamura.

On the way out of the station, Kawamura passed the young clerical staff member.

"Any results?" he asked.

The clerical staff member sucked wind and looked down at his desk.

"I have been told that the tennis club case is closed," he said. "But," he added, looking up, "all the major newspapers were informed about the connection between the suicide in Ueno and our case at the tennis club by anonymous phone calls. Also," added the clerk, "the lipstick on the cigarette butt in the Manabe apartment is different . . . Helene Curtis Passion Flower."

"Mild Seven brand?"

"Mild Seven brand," confirmed the clerk.

"Wonderful," said Kawamura.

"I'm sorry I ever heard about the Tokyo Lawn Tennis Club," said Kawamura as he and Suzuki-san seated themselves on the stools. They were in a beer bar just off the sidewalk in the trendy Roppongi area. Trendy couples surrounded them.

"And now we've been removed from the case," he added.

"Really?" asked Suzuki-san.

"Really," confirmed Kawamura.

"I mean, really?" asked Suzuki-san again.

"Well, really. The case is closed," confirmed Kawamura. Kawamura and Suzuki-san ordered large drafts.

"Chief Arai was *told* that the case was closed," said Suzuki-san after the beers were set down in front of them.

"How do you know?"

"His secretary is a friend of mine," said Suzuki-san taking a deep drink. "And she doesn't miss anything."

Kawamura took a drink of his beer.

"Actually, I'm going to continue . . . looking into it . . . during my vacation."

"Does Chief Arai know that?" asked Suzuki-san.

"Hmm," explained Kawamura.

Suzuki-san finished his beer in three gulps and ordered another one.

"I can help, of course . . . "

"Unofficially," interjected Kawamura.

"Of course, unofficially."

Trendy couples were entering the joint by the minute.

"I wonder who had connections that were powerful enough to stop the investigation?" asked Suzuki-san.

"I don't know. Manabe-san's memoirs may have told us something. We may never get them now," said Kawamura.

Kawamura and Suzuki-san had to squeeze

closer together on their stools to make room for trendy couples.

"Do you know anything about computers?" asked Suzuki-san after Kawamura had ordered another beer.

"Not really. Only what my kids have taught me. Do you know anything about them?"

"Almost nothing," said Suzuki-san. Despite the air conditioning, he was sweating in his blue serge suit.

"Why do you ask?" Kawamura inquired.

Trendy couples were now standing behind the bar and ordering drinks over the shoulders of seated patrons. Despite the fact that it was a beer bar, many of the drinks were in the Campari-soda and orange-blossom-rum category.

"Because of this," answered Suzuki-san, reaching into the inside pocket of his jacket. "These things are somehow important in the operation of those machines."

Suzuki-san flopped a floppy disk on the bar. A trendy couple behind him ordered banana-and-gin floats.

"I found it," Suzuki-san amplified, "inside the computer in Manabe-san's hole."

CHAPTER 23

"It won't work, Papa."

"Won't work? Is something wrong with it?"

Kawamura was in consultation on high technology with his twelve-year-old son.

"I mean my machine and the disk, they're not compatible."

"Can we get it fixed?"

Young Ichiro Kawamura looked at his father. Adults always seemed to have all the answers, but he found there were occasional, and ridiculous, blind spots.

"No, Papa. My machine is designed for . . . "

"You don't have to print anything. I'll just read it on your game screen."

"Display screen," corrected young Ichiro. "If you buy me the new 2400 Series then I can . . . ."

"Never mind, son, I'll get it done at the, ah, office."

Kawamura's son bounded back into his room and the booming rock music as his wife entered with a tray and teacups.

"Did you make arrangements for a day off?" she asked. "These discounts to Disneyland expire at the end of the month."

"Uh, not yet. I'm working on it."

"But that case you were working on is finished. The man with no enemies. I saw in the papers that his best friend did it, then committed suicide."

"There still are . . . loose ends," Kawamura explained.

"Loose ends? You always used to say that your staff worried about loose ends."

"Well, we have a personnel shortage now. Many people are taking . . . "

Kawamura stopped, but it was too late.

"Vacations," said Noriko Kawamura slamming the tray on the table. "And I'll bet *they* are taking their families to Disneyland. A promise made is a . . . "

"I know, I know," said Kawamura impatiently.

He and his wife drank their tea in silence.

CHAPTER 24

Kawamura and Suzuki-san met Thursday morning at a coffee shop across the street and around a corner from the Azabu Police Station.

"Sorry I'm late," said Suzuki-san as he eased the blue serge suit into a tiny chair. "How's your vacation going?"

"That's not funny," said Kawamura. "Here, take

this disk and get the stuff on it printed. I can't do it on my son's machine."

"Why?"

"That's not funny either. And I don't think you should take it back to the station for the printing."

"I understand," said Suzuki-san, putting the disk into his pocket. "I have a friend who has a friend . . ."

"I don't think just anybody should read whatever's on there. We don't know . . ."

"Don't worry. What are your plans today?" asked Suzuki-san.

"Well, since I can't make appointments officially, I thought I might just drop in on a few people."

"Do you want me to go with you?"

"No, that would be too official. What I want from you now more than anything is Manabe-san's memoirs printed out on real paper."

"You'll call me at the station?"

"Several times," promised Kawamura.

Kawamura did nothing more complicated than walk in off the street at Pan-Pacific Property Development Company. The president of the company was Hanada-san, Shig Manabe's distant relative. Hanada was not available, Kawamura was told, and Kawamura could imagine him working on his tan in his Nike outfit at the Tokyo Lawn Tennis Club.

Nat Forrest, Discoverer of the Body, *was* in.

"What a surprise to see you here," said Forrest

in English as Kawamura was shown to his tiny cubicle. "I'm afraid that Mr. Hanada is not here right now."

"That is not a problem," said Kawamura. "I just . . . had the chance to be in this territory, and I saw the company name, so I . . . "

"Can I ask you a question, Captain?" asked Forrest.

"Ask *me* a question? I guess so."

"The English side of your business card says 'Tim' Kawamura. How did you get the name 'Tim'?"

"Well, it's not my *real* name . . . I mean, it's a name designed for foreigners. Americans particularly. To make it easier for them . . . for you."

"How did you learn English, Captain?" asked Forrest, genuinely interested.

"My English is no good," stated Kawamura. "But I learned it as a little boy. I liked to read English mystery stories."

"Mysteries?" Forrest laughed. "And now you're a policeman. I used to read science fiction . . . "

"And now you work for a Japanese company. How did that happen?" asked Kawamura.

"I like the country, and the experience is good for me."

"What do you do here?"

"Pan-Pacific develops property both here and in the States for investors. I guess you could say I'm their 'international expert.' I report on the tax situation for them, supervise the flow of money internationally, and help with their investments."

"Now that the 'bubble' has burst . . . "

"You're right," said Forrest. "Business is terrible."

"Your boss, Hanada, must not be in a good mood these days."

Nat Forrest lowered his voice slightly.

"We just had to release six negotiators, and . . ."

"Negotiators?" Kawamura was not familiar with the term as used in English."

"The people who go around and, ah, convince property owners to sell."

Kawamura understood what Forrest was talking about. The negotiators were pretty tough characters.

"There isn't much new development of golf courses now," said Forrest continuing.

"Would you say Hanada had a . . . short temper?" Kawamura knew he wasn't being very subtle—particularly for an unofficial interview—but he also didn't want to spend the day listening to the problems of property developers.

"He has problems," said Forrest after a moment, but I've never seen him really angry. Except," he added, "when it had to do with his wife."

"His wife?"

"His wife," confirmed Forrest. "She is younger than him . . . I think it's his second wife . . . and he is very jealous."

Forrest smiled briefly thinking about it.

"It's so unlike a Japanese," he finally said. "Yelling like that on the telephone."

Kawamura was having a difficult time keeping the interview tone unofficial.

"Do you have any idea," he asked conversationally, "who would chase after his wife?"

"I have no idea," answered Forrest, "but I *do* think she's chase-able."

"Did you ever . . . ?"

"Me? No. I just got engaged," said Nat Forrest proudly. "I don't run after women like that."

"Yes, I understood you just got engaged. Congratulations. One of the, er, employees at the tennis club."

"One of the waitresses," said Forrest. "A nice girl. Shig Manabe actually introduced us."

"Really?"

"Yes, he said she was very good."

Kawamura and Forrest looked at each other across the small desk. There really was no reason to continue hanging around. Forrest did not seem to know anything more than what he said. It was a charming but sometimes naive trait in Americans. Kawamura stood up.

"I'm sorry Mr. Hanada isn't here," said Forrest, "but I'll tell him you stopped by."

"No, don't do that. As I said, I was just in the territory."

Forrest walked Kawamura to the front door of the office.

"I'm afraid I overreacted at the club last Saturday. Finding Shig that way in the bath."

"It was a natural reaction," said Kawamura.

"But at least the mystery is over."

"Could you have imagined Sakai doing something like that? I mean, you played with Manabe-san . . . "

Forrest stopped by the door.

"Shig would play with me now and then," said Forrest. "He was one of the few people I knew at the club. I know Mr. Hanada, of course, but I'm an employee. I think it was the jealousy thing."

"The jealousy thing?"

"Yeah. Like we were talking about with Mr. Hanada and his wife. I don't mean a sexual thing. I just mean the kind of jealousy people have for each other's time. Sakai-san always wanted to play with Shig. Patterns get established, and it then becomes difficult . . . I guess I'm not explaining it very well."

"If jealousy's the case," said Kawamura, "why didn't Sakai wait until you were in the bath?"

Forrest stopped in the process of opening the door for Kawamura.

"Jesus, Tim, I never thought of that."

It was a very warm day, and Kawamura decided to have an early lunch. He took a taxi across town to the site of Manabe-san's hole—Suzuki's yakitori restaurant. It was not a pleasant way to spend one of his few official holidays, and it would certainly be cooler out at Tokyo Disneyland, but Kawamura soldiered on. Chief Arai's reaction to things *had* been interesting.

Unfortunately, Suzuki the restaurateur had very little to add to the puzzle. He and Manabe-san had first met during the Occupation. Manabe-san was something of a big shot doing translations and other esoteric things while Suzuki was a supply clerk working for the American PX system.

"I used to tell Shig," said Suzuki, "that his future was golden. He knew all the right people. He would tell me that I should go to school to improve myself."

Kawamura ate around the edges of a chicken wing. Suzuki was making the mistake of not serving gizzards in his restaurant.

"And Shig did very well. The pearl business."

Suzuki put a roasted potato on Kawamura's plate.

"But I own this place, the places on either side, and the place across the street. Plus the apartment building in Azabu. Counting our new house in Takanawa, the supply clerk business wasn't all that bad."

Suzuki winked. Kawamura burned his mouth on the roasted potato.

Kawamura left Suzuki's restaurant and walked back into the high-rent district of Azabu and Hiroo Towers. He hoped to have a few moments of conversation with Mrs. Manabe. Presumably, she knew Shig better than anybody.

Kawamura had just entered the plush lobby of the apartment building when he ran into Tatsuo Morimoto. The man was leaving the elevators.

"What are *you* doing here?" the tennis club president asked.

"Well, I'm on holiday, but I thought I'd stop in and . . . see if there's anything I can do."

Morimoto was looking at him, and Kawamura could feel the former ambassador examining his blue suit and tie.

"Holiday?"

"Yes. Mrs. Manabe might need help . . . "

"I don't think you should see her. A doctor has just given her sedatives, and I can confirm that she should not have visitors now," said Morimoto.

"I'm glad to hear things are under control," said Kawamura turning and walking toward the lobby entrance with Morimoto. "She seems like such a nice lady."

Kawamura and Morimoto left the building. Morimoto climbed into a new Mercedes-Benz.

"Can I give you a ride anywhere, Captain Kojima?" asked Morimoto.

"Kawamura," said Kawamura. "And since this is a holiday for me, I'll just go over and catch the subway home. I'm taking the family to Disneyland."

"Good idea," said Morimoto slowly driving away.

Kawamura continued walking toward the shopping area looking for a telephone. He could always go back and visit Mrs. Manabe later.

Kawamura found a telephone and learned that Suzuki-san had already obtained a hard-copy printout of Shig Manabe's memoirs.

"Has anybody looked at them?" asked Kawamura.

"Looked at them? Maybe. Read them, no. It's all in English," said Suzuki-san.

Kawamura and Suzuki-san arranged to meet in the Highlander Bar at the Okura Hotel. Kawamura knew that the place would be virtually deserted, except for a sprinkling of foreigners, after lunch hour.

"How has your day been?" asked Suzuki-san when he arrived. Kawamura brought him up-to-date with a depressingly short report.

"It's better than my day so far," said Suzuki-san. "I've been assigned to writing up summaries of the yakuza attempt to take over apartment buildings in the Juban."

"Don't lose sleep over it," advised Kawamura. "That'll be going on long after we're retired."

"Here are the memoirs," said Suzuki-san, handing over two large manila envelopes. "What do you do now?"

"Sit here and read."

"Call me later," said Suzuki-san rising to leave.

"Several times," agreed Kawamura.

CHAPTER 25

Introduction

I have been lucky all my life. My father was a university graduate and had a good job. My mother was a very refined lady originally from Kyoto. Theirs was a love marriage—they met in a tea house—not one arranged in the Japanese fashion by go-betweens.

My parents married and settled in Yokohama in 1923. A month after the wedding the Great Kanto Earthquake struck, killing many of their neighbors. My father had foreign friends at the Yokohama Country and Athletic Club, and they brought extra food to my parents. The photograph we had of my father with his English friends was one of the few things that survived the war.

I was born two years later. My first memories involved walking up and down the hill from the Bluff. It seemed like a mountain then, but it's nothing now.

The move to Seattle, Washington, in the United States was obviously the biggest thing in my young life. I did not want to go, but my father insisted. I don't think my mother wanted to go either, but my father insisted. It turns out to have been the best thing he ever did.

Kawamura ordered a beer from a waiter in the Highlander Bar. The waiter delivered it with a small dish of peanuts.

> The time I spent in Seattle was for me an eye-opening experience. I realized that students were actually people, and could ask questions in class. I was very sorry to leave there in 1942, but Japan and the United States were at war. The people at the American school were very nice, and gave me an award for playing on their baseball team. I still have it.
>
> My experiences during the war were painful, but I've tried to be fair and to present an honest report of what I saw. The same is true for the years immediately after the war.
>
> My new life in the United States after the University of Michigan may not have been as dramatic, but I did meet many kinds of people— some were wonderful, some were terrible. Fortunately, I was able to succeed at business and to be a small factor in the challenge of bringing international understanding to people who would not normally think that way.
>
> I make no apologies about what follows. I have never meant to hurt people, but if that happens as a result of my recollections, I ask only that the reader consider this: My only strength in life has been to be completely honest at all times.

Kawamura ordered another beer. It was going to be a long afternoon. And he was on vacation anyway.

The first thirty pages dwelled upon the Yokohama years. The only thing Kawamura recognized was an indirect reference to what must have been Sakai.

Tak-chan and I were forced to continue our tennis lessons. His mother and my father insisted upon it. In our point of view, it was a sissy's game. The other boys would see us in our white "western" pants and chase us. Once, caught in a narrow lane with no way out, Tak-chan picked up a rock and hit one of the boys in the middle of his forehead. He nearly bled to death, and we were in big trouble at home.

The years in Seattle were interesting, but something that Kawamura could not really relate to. It appeared that Manabe-san had been picked on by the other kids at school, and his first year in America had been miserable. A physical education instructor had apparently taken an interest in Shig, and he rated several paragraphs in the Manabe memoirs.

Speed McCoy—I never did know what his given name was—took me aside in gym class one day and told me that I was not trying hard enough. He forced me to play catch with him, using what they called a medicine ball. Bigger than a basketball, it weighed four or five kilograms. I played with him until I thought my arms would fall off.

Later, Speed convinced me to go out for the baseball team. Fortunately, with Speed's coaching, I managed to do well. Our junior high school team was undefeated, and I was something of a hero with the highest batting average. For years I've remembered Speed's lesson: If you can do one thing very well, people will respect you.

The return to Japan in 1942 was sudden. Apparently Shig's father had had some idea that the international situation was deteriorating. He had insisted that the family pack their bags and get ready for a sudden departure at least a week before the Pearl Harbor incident.

I think it was Speed McCoy who convinced the school to present me with my baseball letter before the sports banquet. We had an assembly, and they gave it to me. Not everybody was my friend—parents of some of my classmates did not like me—but at least my teammates were on my side. I'll never forget it.

Kawamura had just ordered another beer when the bartender announced that there was a phone call for a Captain Kawamura. Kawamura accepted it, to the bartender's surprise. It was Suzuki-san.

"Yes I'm still here. That's why you're talking to me," explained Kawamura.

There was a pause while Kawamura and the bartender stared at each other.

"OK," said Kawamura into the phone. "I'll be here."

I really had to be careful back in Japan. My father encouraged me to speak English at home whenever the maids were away, but at all other times English was forbidden. A girl I knew, who

was the daughter of my parents' friends, attended Seishin School, which was kept open for
a few years during the war. One time someone
saw her walking home from school with an
English textbook. Japan's secret police—the
Kempeitai—visited her family. They found more
English books in the house, and eventually the
family was moved to Karuizawa "for protection."
My father did not want that to happen to our
family.

Kawamura thought back on his own years after
the war. He had no idea at the time what went on
before, but he remembers his mother being given
a set of Agatha Christie books by an American
who had been assigned to their house in the first
years of the Occupation. Kawamura was just
starting school then, but he now realized how
unusual those books must have been at the time.

My father was too old for the war, and he was
assigned by the War Ministry to the job of
securing parts for the fighter planes being built
by Mitsubishi. He traveled quite a bit in those
days, and we would only see him three or four
times a month. His job was to make sure the
subcontracting machine shops were working at
maximum efficiency for the war effort.

It is ironic that one of our relatives turned my
father in to the Kempeitai. They must have
known that my father had been stationed over-
seas, but there was no problem at first. By the
middle of 1943 it became obvious to some in
Japan that the war was not going as well as
planned. Before he was taken away, my father
mentioned he had said that "Japan has problems" to one of his cousins. The Fujii clan were

lower class, and our side of the family didn't like them, but there were no distinctions in class during the war. Those were hard times, and maybe they did it for the money, but I never saw my father again after that. We never knew what happened to him.

Kawamura made a note to check on Hanada's mother's maiden name. It was a long shot, but at least Kawamura knew there was a family connection. Kawamura also ordered another beer.

The next twenty pages dealt with Shig Manabe's induction into the Imperial Army and his attempts to feign ignorance of English but at the same time demonstrate that he was capable of mastering the enemy's tongue. Manabe-san walked a tightrope that was at times comical.

The instructor lectured me and said that "We want complete information from you" was wrong. The instructor insisted that the correct way to say it was "The information from you complete we must have." I agreed without arguing.

Suzuki-san arrived and immediately ordered a beer. Kawamura looked at his watch and was surprised to find that it was five o'clock.

"Is there anything there?" asked Suzuki-san, referring to the memoirs.

"I don't know. I'm only up to Manabe-san's graduation from high school."

"Women?"

"Not yet. He's probably too young," said Kawamura.

"I have a theory about that," said Suzuki-san. He was still sweating in his blue serge suit. "I went over to the Tokyo Lawn Tennis Club this afternoon."

"You shouldn't have done that," said Kawamura with some concern. "The official investigation is over. Chief Arai may get in trouble . . . "

"Don't worry. I went as a private citizen," said Suzuki-san. "I'm in love."

"What?"

"I'm in love," confirmed a sweating Suzuki. "It can happen to anybody."

Kawamura looked at his assistant's shaved, bullet head.

"You don't realize," added Suzuki-san, "but many ladies like my style. Kojak," he said, referring to an American television show popular in Japan.

"Who are you in love with?" asked Kawamura.

"The waitress," replied Suzuki-san. "She's a wonderful woman named Yamazaki."

"You mean the one who . . . ?"

"Yes, Manabe-san's friend."

"And is engaged to . . . ?"

"Yes, the foreigner. The Discoverer of the Body."

"Suzuki-san . . . "

"And I think we've eliminated half the suspects from the club."

Suzuki-san pulled a small plastic package from his pocket. He opened the package and laid a cigarette butt on the table. It had lipstick on it.

"I had to make a date for next Tuesday night."

"What are you talking about?" asked Kawamura.

"It's my cigarette."

"You don't smoke."

"Manabe-san did," replied Suzuki-san. "And for the sake of the experiment, so did I."

Kawamura stared at Suzuki-san.

"I did what Manabe-san probably did. Kissed her, then smoked a cigarette. It was *his* cigarette in the men's locker room. Miss Yamazaki uses Estée Lauder. We discussed it next to the clubhouse where the beer is delivered."

"But the cigarette butt in Manabe-san's apartment . . . ?"

"Helene Curtis, I know. I plan to visit Mrs. Hanada tomorrow," said Suzuki-san. "Investigative work is not easy," he added.

Kawamura looked at his assistant, then wondered how many men had been caught because of kissing a mistress wearing lipstick then smoking afterwards. It was a point to consider, he concluded.

"Well, I'm not sure I approve of your methods," said Kawamura, "but if you're right, it simplifies things."

"Simplifies things," repeated Suzuki-san. "Are you absolutely certain that the simplest explanation is *not* true? It would be easier *if* Sakai really did it, then . . . "

"That's the problem," said Kawamura. "That's too simple. I still have no theory, but maybe the memoirs . . . "

"What else should I do?" asked Suzuki-san.

"Go into the office the first thing in the morning and see if you can find out if our friend Hanada has relatives named Fujii . . . maybe on his mother's side of the family."

"That'll be easy. I'll ask Mrs. Hanada when I see her tomorrow."

"Remember, this is unofficial," reminded Kawamura.

"You're telling me?" responded Suzuki-san.

Kawamura decided to stay in the Highlander Bar for a half-hour or so after Suzuki-san left. The seat was comfortable, and although the place was beginning to fill up, there was enough space between tables for some degree of privacy. Besides, and most importantly, Kawamura did not wish to return home too early. He was on vacation, but not on vacation.

It was hot when we arrived in Shanghai but it was raining. I will never forget my feeling of horror as we marched with our equipment from the boat to where the trucks were waiting along the street. Thousands of people seemed to be living on the streets or in the destroyed shells of buildings. Combined with what seemed to be steam rising from the cement and bricks, the smell of rot and human waste was almost too much to bear. I couldn't catch my breath, and for a few moments I was afraid I would suffocate. I purposely dropped my pack, then bent over slowly to retrieve it. I did not want anyone to see the tears in my eyes, but I guess with all the rain no one would have noticed anyway.

Manabe and twenty-three of his translating colleagues were sent first to a camp northwest of the city.

> I remember the mud more than anything else. Everywhere we walked there was mud. If we didn't tie our boots correctly, they'd be sucked off by the mud as we walked. Another impression stays with me to this day. Having lived on the West Coast of the United States, and of course in Japan, I had never in my life been any place where there were absolutely no trees—as far as the eye could see. It seemed unnatural to me.

Kawamura looked up from the manuscript and tried to visualize the scene. He had seen photographs from the war years, and had seen movies, but pictures do not convey the smells and the actual feelings. Kawamura had never felt particularly deprived at having no military experience, and Manabe's memoirs were effectively confirming that impression.

> Our barracks were on low ground, which meant all the water, and even some garbage, ran down to where we were. We had to keep our packs and our shoes on the cots with us when we slept. We were there six days, and I was not dry six seconds. It was the only time I thought I should have joined the regular infantry. They got the barracks on the high ground.

Kawamura read on for another dozen pages. An interesting thing was that Manabe apparently never knew for sure just where he was. Some of his translating colleagues stayed in the Shanghai area, some went north, and some were eventually sent south.

> We climbed into the back of the trucks and were told we were going south. My friend Miyabe asked where we were going, and got no answer. I felt like we were prisoners of war. I recognized the names of some of the bigger cities— Hangchow and Nanping—but the rest of it was all a mystery.

Although this was interesting, Kawamura realized that other than a reference to a family named Fujii—that may have turned in his father to the secret police—there was nothing that seemed relevant to Manabe's murder. There were the normal gripes and complaints about senior officers, but those senior officers were probably dead now. And if murder were involved, it would have been Manabe and his colleagues committing mayhem on the senior officers.

Kawamura looked at his watch and was surprised to discover that it was eight o'clock. He gathered up the manuscript papers, paid the bar bill, and hurried off to a train station. He had been concerned about arriving home too early, and now he would be arriving home too late. Why, Captain Kawamura asked himself, am I always in trouble?

CHAPTER 26

The Kawamura family dinner had just finished as Kawamura walked in the front door.

"Hello, Papa," said his daughter as she scooted into her room for a session of heavy metal.

"Did you get a printout?" asked his son.

"Printout? Oh, I see. Yes, I, ah, programmed it."

"*You* did?"

"Of course," said Kawamura. "It was easy."

Kawamura's son repaired to his room and classic rock.

"I called the station today," said Kawamura's wife. Kawamura sensed that Noriko was not in the best of moods. "They said you were on vacation," she added.

"Well, er, it's the younger staff we're getting now days. Since many people are on vacation, they must have assumed that I am too. It's sloppy. I'll talk to them . . . tomorrow."

"You promised . . . "

"I know, I know. Chief Arai already authorized some time off."

Although Kawamura was anxious to get back to Manabe-san's memoirs, an hour or so with Noriko in front of the TV seemed advisable. They watched a quiz show.

"That foreigner, Bitman-san, sounds just like us," observed Noriko. Theodore Bitman had just guessed correctly that the tubelike affair with a rubber balloon on the end was what Basque shepherds used to impregnate sheep. Everyone in the TV studio was falling apart laughing.

"He was a missionary. He learned Japanese before he even came to Japan."

"How do you know?"

"I, ah, read it somewhere," said Kawamura. Bitman's chattering was giving him a headache.

Kawamura was able to get to the manuscript for another hour while his wife did dishes. Manabe was eventually stationed in a prisoner-of-war camp primarily composed of English-speaking captives in Kwangtung Province. Many of the prisoners were British, some were Australians, New Zealanders, and Americans.

You can imagine my surprise when I saw Speed McCoy. He was a pilot, and he had been shot down off the coast near Swatow. He had some injury to his chest, and he was having a hard time breathing. I may have changed a lot during the last two and a half years, but he had changed so much I hardly recognized him. He could barely pick up his head, let alone a medicine ball. My job was to get him to tell us where he flew from and how many other airplanes were there. It was during this time that I first met Moto-san, and I can remember the night that I vowed to myself I would kill him.

Noriko Kawamura wanted to go to bed. Since the children occupied the two bedrooms—for privacy while studying for examinations during the school year—Kawamura and his wife slept on futons in the living-dining room.

Moto-san, Kawamura thought. I've heard that name in connection with this damn case. Unfortunately, Kawamura's notes were back in the station.

"Please move," Noriko said for the third time. "Are you so interested in your work that you can't hear?"

Kawamura snapped back to the present and helped his wife in the procedure of preparing the bedding—a job that meant moving the table to the side of the room and then staying the hell out of the way.

"I'll be reading for a while," said Kawamura after everything was settled. "Reading for a while" in the Kawamura household meant going into the bathroom.

> You may think that my feelings about Moto-san were extreme, but conditions in war are extreme. I used to give Speed some of my rations of food. He was so weak that I was afraid he would die otherwise.
>
> Moto-san caught me doing that one night. He was a member of the Kempeitai, but he was only a year or two older than I. Moto-san brought me back to where they all stayed and began to interrogate me. At one point he held a gun to my head and demanded to know why I was "comforting" the American dog. I couldn't

tell him, and then he pulled the trigger. I heard the click. The gun was empty. But it was too late, I had already messed my pants. I was humiliated, and everyone laughed.

They stopped feeding Speed after that. He died two days later. When I got back to the camp, the other prisoners looked at me. I think they knew my position, but no one could say anything for fear of the Kempeitai. Speed had helped me in my life, and he was the prisoners' friend too. I went outside the camp, threw up, and then decided to kill Moto-san.

Kawamura tip-toed through the living-dining room to the kitchen and the phone.

"Ah, hello, Mrs. Suzuki," Kawamura whispered. "Is your husband still . . . ? Yes, Mrs. Suzuki, I do know what time it is."

Kawamura hadn't the foggiest idea what time it was, but Suzuki-san would understand.

"Suzuki-san," said Kawamura when his worthy assistant got to the phone, "who is Moto-san? I've heard the name during the tennis club investigation."

The pause was short.

"The head of the kitchen?" exclaimed Kawamura. "Mrs. Moto . . . who said Manabe was slow to pay his bills? How old is she?"

The pause was even shorter.

"Late sixties? Is her husband still alive?" asked Kawamura, his voice ranging dangerously high in his sleeping household.

The pause was the shortest yet.

"OK," instructed Kawamura, "the first thing in

the morning I want you to find out how and when he died."

Kawamura knew that Suzuki-san would understand the late-night intrusion. He wasn't sure about Suzuki-san's wife, or his own wife for that matter. Noriko was now awake and wondering why Kawamura was screaming into the telephone.

It seemed to be the thing to do to lie down for a while. Kawamura crawled into his futon next to his wife and tried to go to sleep. His struggle in this regard lasted for about ten minutes. He finally gave up and tiptoed back into the bathroom.

Manabe had not gotten around to killing Moto-san yet. A dozen pages later, the Kempeitai man showed up again as the Japanese camp authorities were surrendering. Speed McCoy had been dead for six months.

> Most of our group could not believe that the Emperor had instructed us to surrender. There were rumors about giant bombs which had been dropped on Hiroshima and Nagasaki, and these must have made a difference. Although our condition was not much better than our prisoners', it was unthinkable that Japan would lose the war. My father's words—"Japan has problems"—came back to me. I wondered what the Kempeitai thought now.

Kawamura's daughter wanted to use the toilet. Kawamura stood outside and listened to his wife's steady breathing. When his daughter had finished, Kawamura went back into the "reading room."

We were told to assemble outside our barracks and stand at attention. Our camp commander, General Tokura, was to read a statement that confirmed our surrender. It was strange, we would be surrendering to an American lieutenant who had been brought into the camp as a prisoner only a month before. I had interviewed him. He was a Chicago Cubs fan.

As we were getting ready to go outside—and keep in mind that surrendering is not something people hurry to do—Moto-san came into our room looking for me. He said, in front of everybody, that Japan lost the war because of people like me. I don't know about that, but I *was* Japanese, I still *am* Japanese, and I always did what I was told to do.

I picked up a pipe that we used to prop up a window—I had never done this kind of thing before—and hit him with it in the middle of his face.

Kawamura's son wanted to use the toilet. Kawamura stood outside and listened to his wife's steady breathing. Fortunately, she was still sleeping deeply.

When his son had finished, Kawamura went back into the "reading room"—this time sitting on the wooden boards that covered the bath.

There was blood all over his face. He tried to grab me, but I ducked away. I was surprised he was still able to move. I remember tripping over a corner of a bunk and falling backwards. I heard the explosion before I felt it. Moto-san had pulled his gun—which he was about to surrender—and shot me. The bullet went through the bottom of my boot and out the top. I still think about it every time I look at my toe, but I guess I'm lucky to be alive. The other enlisted men grabbed Moto-san and beat him senseless.

Kawamura's wife wanted to use the toilet. Kawamura stood outside and thought about the memoirs. Manabe had vowed to kill the Kempeitai man, but so far all he had done was get into a barracks-room brawl with him. Sakai may have been right. Shig Manabe preferred to sway with the wind instead of taking a definite stand. As a policeman, Kawamura found this to be exemplary. As a flesh-and-blood man, Kawamura found this to be puzzling.

Manabe's memoirs were maddeningly silent over the next period regarding the fate of Moto-san. The text was full of names of people Manabe had worked with during the Occupation—bizarre foreign names like Ingrassia, Conboy, Harezlak, Phelan, Misevich, and Bruscato. The people behind these names were now half a world away from the Tokyo Lawn Tennis Club and the events of last weekend. Some of Manabe's relationships with the names were pleasant, some were less so. But nowhere was there a lead or a clue that Kawamura could see.

He skipped on to the University of Michigan period of Shig Manabe's life.

> I arrived in Ann Arbor without knowing a soul. I did have one name to contact, a Professor Glynn, and he took me under his wing. We went out drinking my first night in town, and I was sick for the next three days.

There were more foreign names, and several references to the fact that a number of students were on the G. I. Bill.

> I never knew what to expect whenever I met an older student. Some of them had fought against Japan and were still angry. Some of them didn't seem to care.

Kawamura did find one name from the past. Manabe was referring to a student he would meet every Wednesday morning as he was changing classes.

> We passed on the sidewalk each Wednesday for a couple of months and never acknowledged each other. He looked familiar to me, and I think I must have looked familiar to him. One day he stopped me and said the name of the prison camp. Then I knew. His name was Keating, and he was in the camp at the time Speed McCoy died. I went out drinking with him that night, and we became somewhat friendly—although he still hated Japan.

Kawamura was becoming groggy. His watch

was outside, next to the futon, but he guessed it was around three in the morning. He skipped ahead to the point where Manabe became involved in the pearl business. He could always go back and read about the Manabe-Caplan wedding later.

Kawamura almost missed it. Words were beginning to blur, but he looked again. Miyabe. That name?

Kawamura went back and found it in the manuscript:

> My friend Miyabe asked where we were going, and got no answer.

Miyabe was the guy on the truck when the translators were being sent out of Shanghai. But Miyabe was also the first employee of the pearl business in Japan.

> He would fly to New York four times a year with a price list from the suppliers. We would review it, sometimes make counteroffers, and he would go back and negotiate. It was a good system at the time, but eventually our suppliers knew what we expected and what we would pay for. As things in the market stabilized, it became unnecessary to have Miyabe doing the face-to-face negotiations. Shirley and our accountants strongly advised me to change the situation. It was difficult dealing with my friend Miyabe on this, but these things happen in business. We offered him something else in Japan, but he refused it. I'm afraid he's never forgiven me.

But it was Kimura—the bookstore inventory clerk with cravats and paisley shirts—who had that job. *He* was the one who rolled around on court number nine fighting Shig Manabe.

Kawamura flipped through the pages of the manuscript.

> The lawsuit with Thomas Backman was particularly painful to me. I had trusted him and loaned him money, but he *did* go into direct competition with us. I understand why he did it, but I was advised that the best thing would be to establish our position and collect on the loan. We settled in a manner that was mutually beneficial.

Clearly, "Thomas Backman" was Theodore Bitman. Did all these people change their names? Kawamura thought about that. Unlikely, he concluded. Shig Manabe, for whatever reasons, had disguised their names. So much for Manabe's introductory statement which read: "My only strength in life has been to be completely honest at all times."

Kawamura stood up and decided it was time for bed. There was something about Shig Manabe he didn't like. He would come close, but never quite deliver the blow.

Kawamura picked up the second envelope containing the manuscript. It contained the last part of the memoirs. Kawamura looked through the material. The last page of text was the one he had quickly glanced at in Manabe's hole. In a writer's method of keeping track of things, the top page was always the last page.

But the disk Suzuki-san found in Manabe's computer contained several pages beyond the last page of printed text. There were acknowledgments and references to documents and sources for detailed information. And there was a dedication: *To Takashi Sakai—who was always brave enough to keep the keys.*

Kawamura had no idea what that meant. And he was tired. He looked at his watch next to the futon as he lay down and was surprised to find that it was four-thirty.

He slept fitfully. The phrase that Mrs. Manabe and Suzuki the restaurateur had claimed Manabe always used kept popping into his mind: "Keys," Manabe had said, "are dangerous."

CHAPTER 27

Kawamura was not at his sparkling best as the household stirred three hours later. He shaved, dressed, and picked his way through a breakfast of soup, pickles, rice, and a tossed green salad.

"Will you know about your vacation schedule today?" asked his wife as he was putting on his shoes at the door.

"I, ah, will confirm it with Chief Arai today,"

Kawamura promised. This whole thing was ridiculous. Kawamura came close to telling his wife what he was doing, but decided against it.

"Remember, a promise . . . "

"I know, I know," confirmed Kawamura. The children were already back into their rooms listening to booms, wailings, and thumps.

Kawamura walked slowly toward the train station. He stopped at a small shop first and had a cup of coffee. It was a miniluxury he never had time for during the normal course of dashing to the Azabu Police Station before nine.

At nine-thirty Kawamura called and asked for Suzuki-san. He was still in the morning meeting, said one of the junior staff members. Chief Arai must be onto a new tangent, thought Kawamura. He paused a moment, then decided to call the Ueno Police Station. The captain he had met there was named Ogishi. It turned out that Captain Ogishi was on vacation. Kawamura explained that he was a colleague and close personal friend since grade-school days, but, he confessed, he had lost "Ogi"-san's home phone number. There was some wind-sucking reluctance from the other end of the line—highly irregular, you understand—but grade-school friends were grade-school friends. Kawamura was given Ogishi's home phone number.

Kawamura called Suzuki-san again, but the morning meeting was still going on. Kawamura then called Captain Ogishi at home.

"I was told to get out of the office and take a few

days off," said Ogishi. "Something about this whole thing smells worse than Sakai's apartment the day we found him."

"I'm in the same situation," admitted Kawamura. "But I'm still looking into it unofficially."

"Good. I've still got my copy of the investigation files. What do you want to do?"

"Was anything found in Sakai's apartment?" Kawamura asked. "I'm thinking about unaccountable keys, and that kind of thing."

"I have no idea. We didn't do a thorough search. At the time . . . "

"I understand," said Kawamura. "Where are his things now?"

"A relative is cleaning out the apartment . . . today, as a matter of fact," said Ogishi.

"I wonder if I could . . . ?"

"It's outside your jurisdiction, Captain," said Ogishi.

"I know, but . . . "

"Just a minute," said Ogishi.

Kawamura could hear muffled conversation as Ogishi spoke to someone with his hand over the phone.

"OK," said Ogishi speaking to Kawamura. "Let's meet at Sakai's apartment in an hour."

"You're sure that's no problem for you?" asked Kawamura.

"Of course not," answered Ogishi. "I was going to take the family to Disneyland, but I can do that tomorrow."

Kawamura expressed profound gratitude and

hung up. There was time for another cup of coffee before calling Suzuki-san again.

When he did get through to the Azabu station and Suzuki-san, there was a trace of panic in his assistant's voice.

"I think there is a big problem," said Suzuki-san, "and I think you should be careful."

"What's the matter? We already know Chief Arai was told . . . "

"The pressure must be worse now. We had to go through every single thing we did in the investigation. Chief Arai went through all the reports, and demanded to be given any photocopies we may have made. He took everything, and I think he went to the Tokyo Metropolitan Police Headquarters."

"Did you tell him about the computer disk?" asked Kawamura.

"It's amazing," answered Suzuki-san, "I forgot about that. But anyway, Chief Arai told me to tell you to *really* take a vacation. In fact I think he tried to catch you at home this morning."

"I must have left already. In any event, I'm going to meet the captain from Ueno and look at some of the things in Sakai's apartment."

Suzuki-san paused. Kawamura could visualize him frowning.

"Are you sure . . . of course it's not my position to say . . . but are you sure that's wise?" asked Suzuki-san. "I mean, Chief Arai seemed very concerned . . . "

"I don't know what's wise in this damn case,

but the guy from Ueno and I are on vacation. We're just concerned citizens."

"What should I do?"

"Absolutely nothing for now," said Kawamura. "And stay away from Mrs. Hanada and her lipstick. The Fujii name may not be the one in her husband's family anyway."

Kawamura briefly explained that Shig Manabe may have changed or disguised names in his memoir.

"Interesting," said Suzuki-san. "Do the memoirs say anything about the yakuza?"

"The yakuza? Not as far as I've read. Why?"

"Our staff told me that Hanada's property development company has some connection with organized crime. I don't understand the details, but something about moving money around."

"Terrific," said Kawamura sourly. "I can't believe we're being compromised by those people, but anyway that's another reason to stay away from Mrs. Hanada. "At least for the time being," Kawamura added.

Kawamura hung up, paid his bill, and picked up his briefcase containing the manuscript. It struck him that Shig Manabe would probably disguise the yakuza as Boy Scouts.

The train Kawamura normally took to the station went to Ueno in the other direction. It was an odd feeling, Kawamura noticed, entering the station as always, but crossing over to the other set of tracks going away from his normal destination. Habits die hard.

Kawamura also noticed, across the tracks on the other platform, the two serious-looking men in dark blue suits pretending to read their papers. They were standing back to back, each staring at one of the two entrances. They were too old for active-duty policemen, Kawamura realized, which meant they were probably private detectives chasing some poor bastard suspected of whatever it is poor bastards are suspected of.

Kawamura's train roared into the station. His mind was focused on keys.

CHAPTER 28

Captain Ogishi of the Ueno Police Station had arrived and was already standing in the doorway of the late Tak Sakai's apartment when Kawamura got there. Ogishi was not pretending to be on duty—he was wearing jeans, a loose-fitting T-shirt, and sneakers.

Inside the apartment, a young man and woman in their late twenties were sorting through the personal effects of the last Silver Fox. It was probably Kawamura's imagination, but despite the airing and obvious disinfectants, the room still had the cloying sweet smell of death. Kawamura wondered if people in other parts of the world were as reluctant as Japanese to rent or purchase apartments in which violent death had occurred.

The young woman, it turned out, was Sakai's niece—his closest relative. She and the young man had been married two months.

"I still can't believe it," she said. "My uncle would not murder his best friend and then kill himself."

"How do you know?" asked Kawamura.

"How do I know?" repeated the young woman. She looked up from a cardboard box containing Sakai's underwear and socks. She was actually quite attractive, Kawamura now noticed, but she also seemed to have the same blustery toughness as her uncle. "I know because we were flesh and blood. I was his closest relative, but he was also *my* closest relative."

The young lady glanced briefly at her new husband who was sorting clothing from the closet into two piles. She stood up, walked to the window, and lit a cigarette. She opened the window slightly and looked down at the street outside.

"My mother was his little sister. She died when the Korean Airlines flight from the United States was shot down by the Russians. I was still a teenager, and . . . confused. Uncle Tak took me in, even though his wife was dying of cancer. He didn't have to do that . . . in fact it was very difficult for him to do that . . . but he did. He was always my special friend, but he really became my friend then."

The young woman looked down at the street,

her husband continued sorting, Ogishi stood by the door.

"I was going to kill myself," she said suddenly, "but he talked me out of it. Nobody could feel the way he did, could say the things he did, and act so differently."

"To be honest, I'm looking for anything . . . ," Kawamura began.

"Do you know what he did during the war?" she interrupted. "He ran away. A man in that day and age . . . ran *away*. He worked as a laborer in Hokkaido. And pretended to be a simpleton. He was a university graduate."

"I understand he didn't like Americans," said Kawamura.

"Hated them," she confirmed. "And you know why? Because of what the war made him do. Run away. But he could never kill anyone . . . including them."

The young woman dropped her cigarette in an empty saké bottle and reached into the pocket of her slacks.

"Captain Ogishi said you were looking for keys. Here they are."

She handed Kawamura a ring containing two keys—one for the apartment, and one most probably for the locker at the Tokyo Lawn Tennis Club. Sixty-eight years on this earth, Kawamura thought, and two keys. There was very little else to say.

Kawamura and Ogishi helped the young couple sort things for another two hours. There were two basic piles—one containing things that would be thrown away, the other containing things that would be donated to charity. A third and very small pile contained personal mementos which the niece would keep. On that third pile was a small photograph that was found lying in the corner under the desk. It was a picture of the niece and her mother. The niece appeared to be about ten years old. She looked even more like Sakai then.

"Is your father still alive?" asked Kawamura.

"No," said the young woman. "He's dead."

Kawamura put on his suit jacket. He and Ogishi were going to lunch.

"My mother never married," said the niece after a moment.

"Oh?" said Kawamura.

"But if anything, he would have killed him then," she added.

"Who?"

"Shig Manabe was my father," said the young woman, lighting another cigarette.

CHAPTER 29

"The normal thing to do would be to adopt her," said Ogishi. He and Kawamura were sitting on the floor of a traditional restaurant which specialized in fried eels served over steaming rice. Since the two men were on vacation, they were drinking saké. "Sakai and his wife had no children, and when she was born . . . "

"I can imagine Sakai's sister being a strong woman, too," said Kawamura, "and maybe she refused. Shig Manabe, who I'm liking less by the minute, probably couldn't. His wife . . . and all that."

"What do you think happened?" asked Ogishi chomping on an eel.

"I don't really know. It could be something simple. In fact, anyone from the tennis club could have done it. Not only that, it's possible someone could have slipped in from the street and killed him. But . . . "

"Sakai," said Ogishi.

"Sakai," agreed Kawamura. "I think he was framed, and I have a feeling Manabe was murdered by someone else to keep him from publishing his memoirs."

"What do you have from those memoirs?" asked Ogishi.

"Nothing, so far. It's an entire book. And I think Manabe was being cute and disguising the real people."

Ogishi swabbed the last piece of eel around the lacquer dish, picking up sauce and remaining grains of rice.

"Well," said Ogishi after satisfying himself that there was nothing edible in front of him, "we have nothing other than what I told you on the phone . . . an injury to his stomach immediately prior to his death, and unbreakable glasses that probably were crushed by someone stepping on them with shoes."

"Not much," observed Kawamura.

"Not much at all," agreed Ogishi. "But that's not what's important. Never in my life have I been called off a case by mysterious influences above me. *That's* the significant thing about this case. Who has the power to do that?"

"That's at my end," said Kawamura.

"I'm afraid so," agreed Ogishi, "but I'm keeping my copy of the report away from the station."

Kawamura picked up the tab, then headed back to the train to the Azabu area. The plan was to give Mrs. Manabe one more shot. She might be able to fill in the blanks regarding the made-up names in her husband's memoirs.

Kawamura called his wife from the station. It was not a comfortable conversation.

"Chief Arai called just after you left this morning and said to tell you to *really* take your vacation," reported his wife. "What does *that* mean, and where are you?"

"It's complicated," Kawamura revealed. "I'll explain when I get home tonight."

"Tonight?" queried Noriko Kawamura. "What's wrong with right now? The children . . . "

"I know, a promise made is a debt unpaid," said Kawamura.

The young lady at the phone next to Kawamura stared at him.

"We'll talk about it tonight," said Kawamura hanging up.

"My homosexual lover," said Kawamura to the young lady at the phone next to him—giving her something to talk about later with her friends.

CHAPTER 30

Kawamura continued looking through Shig Manabe's manuscript as the train roared along underground from Ueno to Azabu. He looked up briefly as the train stopped at the station near his home. The two serious men in blue suits were gone. Either they had found their man or they had given up.

> Making the decision to retire was not the difficult thing I always thought it would be. My wife and I talked about it many times, and since we have no children we decided to let the business run out. Now and then we may fill a special order for an old customer, but most of our previous customers are handled by Tom Backman's company.

The fake name again. Kawamura moaned.

> Although I have many friends in the New York area, I find it enjoyable to spend half my time in Tokyo. My wife accompanies me to

Japan once or twice a year, but she prefers New York. I guess when one gets older, one goes back to days of childhood. In my case, I prefer a simple game of tennis with my life-long friend Tak Sakai.

Kawamura emerged from the station nearest the Manabe apartment. The sun was bright, and if anything it was hotter in this part of town than out in Ueno.

The frustrating thing about the damn memoirs, Kawamura realized, is that Manabe was not honest. He had said he would tell the complete truth, but he refused to acknowledge fathering a child with his old pal's sister. It also appeared that he changed the names of people selectively. Sakai was clearly Sakai, but Backman was Bitman and Miyabe was Kimura. Who or what the other names meant was anybody's guess.

Kawamura entered the lobby of the apartment building. The last time he was there he had run into the tennis club president, former Ambassador Morimoto. It would please Kawamura very much not to run into him again.

Fortunately, Mrs. Manabe was home. She did not sound very pleased on the speaker-phone about visiting with Kawamura, but she buzzed him through the security doors. Upon reaching the thirteenth floor, Kawamura found himself watching for the second time that day the spectacle of a loved one packing belongings after a sudden and tragic death.

"It's time for tea anyway," said Mrs. Manabe in

greeting Kawamura, "so you may as well sit down."

Kawamura found it difficult to question the lady too closely about her late husband. Mrs. Manabe had recovered somewhat from the shock of the last five days, and her answers were more specific and to the point. But Kawamura had to be careful. He did not wish to reveal that he had a copy of the memoirs—something quite illegal, the policeman in him realized—so he must not ask about things he could know only from reading the manuscript.

"No, I didn't find any unusual keys," said Mrs. Manabe, now sitting on the couch and looking morosely at the partially filled cardboard boxes on the floor. "And I've been through everything."

Kawamura looked at the boxes. Putting one's life in boxes suddenly struck him as being very sad.

"Someone at the tennis club," said Kawamura— he did not like lying and he now felt like Shig Manabe—"overheard your husband say that his friend Sakai was 'always brave enough to keep the keys.' Do you have any idea what that might have meant?"

Mrs. Manabe frowned and took several moments before replying.

"I have no idea," she replied at last. "Shig always said 'keys are dangerous,' but that was his way. He was very secretive."

"I just visited Sakai's apartment," said Kawamura. He had decided to see if there was a reaction from Mrs. Manabe. "Sakai's niece was there, but there were not any unusual keys."

Mrs. Manabe did not react, but continued frowning. The teakettle in the kitchen began whistling.

"She was Shig's daughter," announced Mrs. Manabe in a matter-of-fact tone. "She'll be looked after in Shig's will."

She rose and went to the kitchen. Kawamura was shocked. She knew about the child, but wasn't any more bothered by it than discovering an extra and unknown pair of shoes. Did Shig know she knew? And if so, why state in the memoirs that there were no children?

"I, ah, er, didn't . . . ," said Kawamura as Mrs. Manabe returned with two cups of tea on a tray.

"Don't be so surprised, Captain. It was Shig's one weakness. Everyone liked him, and he . . . tended to like everyone. He had a number of affairs. Afterwards, he'd confess and promise . . . "

Mrs. Manabe's voice trailed off. Kawamura was afraid she'd break into tears. He also wondered if she knew about the distant relative's wife and the waitress from the club.

"What is the word for 'key' in Japanese?" asked Mrs. Manabe suddenly. She was frowning again.

"Kagi," replied Kawamura.

"What does that mean to you?"

"It means . . . *kagi* . . . something to unlock a door or a drawer . . . " Kawamura was puzzled by the question. A *kagi* was a *kagi*.

"It can mean something broader in English," said Mrs. Manabe. "A key . . . can unlock a puzzle.

It can be a code. I think *that's* the meaning Shig had in mind."

"A piece of paper?" asked Kawamura, visualizing all the pieces of paper he had just helped Sakai's niece throw away.

"Or just a sequence. Something that can be carried in the head," said Mrs. Manabe. "Shig told me that if something ever happens to him . . . " Mrs. Manabe paused and again seemed on the verge of tears, " . . . if anything happened to him, I should consult with Tak Sakai before publishing the memoirs."

"But why would your husband go to all the trouble of writing the memoirs, in secret and everything, and then change . . . ?"

"You didn't know Shig. He was always very careful. It was his way, he used to say, to survive. He once created an advertising campaign for our company in New York, in secret, but at the last minute he changed one or two things that completely altered the program. He had planned it that way."

"I still don't understand why . . . ," said Kawamura.

"That was Shig's way. His way to survive."

Mrs. Manabe rose from the couch.

"You must excuse me, I have more things to pack. Besides, maybe the men from your station will be able to figure it out. Remember, I want whatever they take returned by tomorrow. I'll be packing that . . . "

"What men?" asked Kawamura, also standing.

"*Your* men. The detectives," answered Mrs. Manabe. "Now that you have a court order to inspect Shig's writing place, I told them how to get to Suzuki's yakitori restaurant."

"Can I use your phone?" Kawamura hoped he didn't appear as concerned as he felt. His assistant, Suzuki-san, confirmed that to the best of his knowledge there was no court order, and in any event no one from the Azabu Police Station would pay a call on Mrs. Manabe without Chief Arai's permission. And he was missing. Kawamura told Suzuki-san to meet him as soon as possible, but without sirens, at Manabe's hole.

"Is anything wrong?" asked Mrs. Manabe.

"I don't know, probably just some bureaucratic confusion," answered Kawamura. "What did these . . . detectives look like?"

"They must have been very senior," replied Mrs. Manabe, "in fact they looked like they were Shig's age. There were two of them, they wore dark blue suits, and . . . that's it."

"Did they show you the court order?"

"Of course. They had it with them. But," added Shirley Manabe, "it was written in Japanese."

CHAPTER 31

Kawamura, his suit jacket over his shoulder,

jogged along the sidewalk in semitropical heat. The yakitori restaurant was too close for a taxi, but the point was academic. There wasn't an empty taxi in sight.

Turning down the narrow street, Kawamura stopped jogging. He walked up to the restaurant slowly, trying to catch his breath while mopping his forehead. He was too late.

Two police cars from the neighboring Shirogane Police Station were wedged into the narrow space. In front of them, obviously the last to arrive, was an ambulance with its red light flashing. Several dozen shopkeepers, neighbors, and passersby stood in the narrow lane and watched.

Kawamura's assistant was already there. Suzuki-san was talking to a policeman in uniform.

"What happened?" asked Kawamura.

"I'm sorry, sir. You can't go in there," said the policeman in uniform.

"It's OK," said Suzuki-san to the policeman. "He's with me."

"I'm with you?"

"I mean," said Suzuki-san, correcting himself to the policeman, "I'm with him."

Conversation was interrupted by two hospital attendants carrying a stretcher out of the restaurant. Wrapped head to foot was an obviously dead body.

"That was Suzuki," said Suzuki-san.

Kawamura and Suzuki-san stepped into the wake of the departing attendants and entered the establishment. Kawamura recognized his counterpart, a captain at the Shirogane station. Although Shirogane and Azabu were separated by one broad street, it was different territory and responsibility.

"It's a surprise to see you here," said the Shirogane captain.

"This is one of my favorite yakitori restaurants," said Kawamura. "What happened?"

The Shirogane captain took Kawamura by the arm and moved to the rear of the restaurant. Suzuki-san wandered off.

"That's his wife over there," said the captain, indicating a sobbing woman being comforted by a lady of approximately the same age. "She was apparently notified by one of the regular customers."

It developed that the routine in the restaurant was for Suzuki to arrive early, clean up things from the night before, and get ready for serving meals at about 11:00 A.M. His wife and one of the daughters would arrive shortly before noon and handle the lunch-hour rush.

After about 2:00 P.M., the ladies would leave and Suzuki would remain in the establishment—sometimes serving meals, sometimes just scrubbing the grills and getting ready for the big business at dinner. Most beer was delivered at this time.

"From what we understand, a regular customer . . . he runs the fish store around the corner . . . came here at about three o'clock for his usual beer and a chicken wing," explained the captain. "He discovered the body at the foot of the stairs."

Kawamura and the captain looked at the foot of the stairs leading up to Shig Manabe's hole.

"He must have tripped and fallen down the steps," added the Shirogane captain. "His neck was broken . . . he died immediately."

"Would you do me a favor?" asked Kawamura. "Would you order a complete autopsy?"

"Well . . . "

"And could I look around? Upstairs, for example?"

"This is more than your favorite yakitori restaurant, isn't it?" asked the captain. "I'd have to put it in my report."

Kawamura noticed Suzuki-san walking down the steps from upstairs.

"Never mind," said Kawamura. "I'm unofficial on this. I don't want to appear in a report."

"Call me later," said the Shirogane captain.

"I will," said Kawamura.

"It was gone," said Suzuki-san.

He and Kawamura had walked out of the immediate neighborhood and back to the Hiroo area near the Manabe apartment. Kawamura was drinking coffee, Suzuki-san was eating a "Chicago" special hot dog with a topping of mustard, relish, onions, cheese, chili beans, jalapeño peppers, corn, and pineapple slices.

"The tray was empty and the cover was off the computer and lying on the floor," continued

Suzuki-san. "It was different from the way we left it."

"Well, whoever they were, they took the manuscript," said Kawamura, "but they probably know the disk is missing."

"I wonder how those people who visited Mrs. Manabe knew about the hole," pondered Suzuki-san between bites.

"It could have been a lucky guess," said Kawamura, "or they could have been tipped off by a copy of my previous reports."

"That would mean someone inside our station, one of the staff, talked," said Suzuki-san. "That would be impossible."

Suzuki-san finished the Chicago hot dog. Kawamura stared at the coffee in his cup. Something about Mrs. Manabe's brief description of the phony detectives rang a bell.

"Do you think it could be the yakuza?" asked Kawamura.

Suzuki-san belched before answering.

"It doesn't seem like their way of doing things," answered Suzuki-san. "They're not . . . subtle. They'd be inclined to walk in and shoot or stab somebody. But staging an accident? I don't think so."

Kawamura nodded in agreement.

"But we should figure out a way to unofficially interview Hanada, the distant relative," said Kawamura. "You said he had underworld connections."

Suzuki-san belched again.

"I could always interview Hanada's wife," suggested Suzuki-san, "and check the lipstick . . . "

"No," said Kawamura. "And that's an order. I don't think Shig Manabe's female entanglements figure in this."

"Do you realize that Chief Arai is not in the office? The rumor is that he's been temporarily removed from duty."

"Because of the murder at the tennis club?"

"I don't know," answered Suzuki-san. "Even his secretary doesn't know."

Kawamura finished his coffee.

"Do you mind coming over to the tennis club with me?" asked Kawamura.

"Of course not. But *should* we? Chief Arai was pretty definite that you should take a vacation."

"Listen, Suzuki-san," said Kawamura standing and picking up the check, "you should learn that in life, promises made are debts unpaid."

"I can't believe you actually say those things," said Suzuki-san walking out the door belching.

CHAPTER 32

It was during the walk up the hill to the tennis club that the light dawned. The two senior detectives who visited Mrs. Manabe *could* have been the two men Kawamura saw at his subway station on the opposite platform that morning.

There were a million men or more in Japan who answered that description, but things had reached an obviously deadly stage. And they probably now knew that a computer disk of the manuscript was missing. If they were on the train platform waiting for him, Kawamura realized they knew where he lived.

Kawamura charged through the entrance doors of the club, ignored the lady at the desk, and immediately went into the manager's office.

"I must use your phone immediately," said Kawamura to the startled manager. It was beginning to get dark, and the staff was wrapping up the business of the day.

Kawamura made two phone calls. The first to the Tokyo Bay Hilton Hotel next to Disneyland. The second to his wife.

"I *know* it's nearly dinnertime. But do as I say. Take the children and go there immediately. There's a reservation in our name. I'll join you when I can."

Noriko Kawamura had only experienced this once before during her marriage. It was when the investigation of loan sharks operating in Roppongi had turned nasty. There had been some vague threats against Kawamura and the other investigating officers. Kawamura and his wife had long ago agreed that anything, no matter how vague, was to be taken seriously when the family was involved. And besides, he was pretty certain he could slip the hotel bill through the accounting department under the heading "investigating expense."

"OK," said Kawamura's wife. There would be no further discussion now. "But please be careful."

"I'll be more careful than I'm probably hired to be," confirmed Kawamura. He firmly believed that getting hurt on the job—including having a fingernail bitten off—was way, way beyond the call of duty.

Kawamura hung up and turned to the startled manager.

"I would like to examine the lockers assigned to Manabe and Sakai."

The manager hesitated a moment before answering. He looked down and shuffled some papers on his desk.

"I'm afraid Manabe-san's locker has already been cleaned out," stated the manager. "One of his distant relatives is a member here and . . . "

"Hanada?"

"Yes, how did you know?" asked the manager. "He said he was helping . . . "

"Did you see what was in the locker?" interrupted Kawamura.

"Tennis things," said the manager trying to be helpful. "What else would there be?"

"We thought some, er, keys. Or paper," answered Kawamura. "Did you look at the tennis things?"

The manager looked down at the papers on his desk and began shuffling again.

"I'm afraid," reported the manager, "that I didn't have time to go up there with Hanada. He is a member, and he was a distant . . ."

"I understand," said Kawamura making an effort to keep calm. "Would you please show us Sakai's locker? I have his key."

"That won't be necessary," said the manager, rising and walking toward the door of the office.

"You have passkeys for all lockers?"

"Yes, of course," said the manager. He went out to the lobby, Kawamura and Suzuki-san followed him up the circular stairs to the locker rooms.

"I'm afraid there is a little puzzle," continued the manager as he reached the top of the stairs and turned left into the men's locker room. "We, ah, didn't report it yet. It could have been an accident."

The men walked along four or five rows of lockers until they came to a bank of lockers against the wall. Everything was surprisingly neat and orderly—except for one locker door along the bank. Out of uniform, it was open.

"We noticed it this morning," said the manager.

Kawamura and Suzuki-san walked over and looked at the locker carefully. The door had been forced open—not a particularly difficult job given the plastic and light metal involved in the locker's construction.

Inside, on the floor of the locker, were a pair of obviously used socks, a pair of jockey underpants, and the remains of a roll of tape. On a shelf near the top was a comb with teeth missing, and an empty bottle of roll-on deodorant.

"Fingerprints?" whispered Suzuki-san to Kawamura.

"Probably not," answered Kawamura. "We couldn't get anyone to come over here anyway. The case is closed."

"Why didn't you report this?" Kawamura asked the manager.

"We didn't think Sakai kept anything valuable here. He used to come with a bag of clean clothes every time he played."

The three men looked at the locker.

"It could have been an accident," said the manager.

"Right," said Kawamura looking at marks probably caused by a screwdriver at the edge of the door. "When did Hanada pick up Manabe-san's things?"

"This morning," replied the manager.

The three men looked at the locker.

"Our plan was to have someone come tomorrow and fix it," said the manager. "There is a waiting list for lockers."

Kawamura nodded, and walked to the doorway of the locker room. He wondered if renting lockers of people who had died violently was as difficult as renting living quarters. Like anything else, it probably depended on price.

At the bottom of the stairway the three men were bid good night by the departing staff. Among them was the waitress, who looked at Suzuki-san for a moment then smiled at Kawamura. Nat Forrest, Kawamura realized, would have his hands full.

CHAPTER 33

"Not there yet?" asked Suzuki-san as Kawamura returned to the table. The two men were dining at a Korean barbecue restaurant in Azabu Juban. The air in the room was blue with smoke.

"Not yet," said Kawamura, "but I know the manager of security at the hotel, and he'll keep his eyes open for them. I'm probably overreacting, but . . . that's the way it goes. What about you?"

Suzuki-san moved pieces of meat around on the grill at their table, his bald head shining with moisture. Kawamura had been introduced to Suzuki-san's "wife" on at least five occasions. On each occasion, Suzuki-san and his "wife" formed a perfect couple—devoted, attentive, and obviously enthralled with each other. Noriko Kawamura even commented on that fact at least three of the times. The problem was each of the wives, all five times, was different. Suzuki-san's domestic arrangements were complex, and Kawamura never felt up to probing too deeply.

"I'm somewhat fluid at the moment," said

Suzuki-san. "I don't think anyone will find me. But I don't think you're overreacting."

"You know, the kids . . . "

"I understand," said Suzuki-san, "but I'd be less concerned about your mysterious men in blue suits than I would be with the bureaucratic problem."

"Chief Arai wasn't home," said Kawamura.

"That's what I mean. I've never seen him so upset. Not the usual thing . . . yelling at us . . . I mean *upset*. He stormed out of the office after his meeting with the Tokyo Metropolitan big shots."

Kawamura and Suzuki-san ate for several minutes in silence. Of particular interest was the cabbage sautéed in garlic accompanying the grilled meat. It made Kawamura's eyes water. Suzuki-san appeared to be unaffected by the power inherent in that particular dish.

"The yakuza? Something to do with the distant relative Hanada?" asked Kawamura.

Suzuki-san ordered more of the cabbage from a passing waitress.

"As I said before," Suzuki-san announced after a belch, "activities involving the yakuza tend to be crude. This whole thing, sneaking around here and there, doesn't seem to fit."

Kawamura speared a potato which turned out to be a garlic clove from the grill.

"I tend to agree," Kawamura said. "And I can't imagine someone like Chief Arai bowing to pressure in that regard. But what else could it be?"

"What do the memoirs say?" asked Suzuki-san.

Kawamura looked down at the briefcase he'd been carrying around for the last two days.

"Nothing yet. I haven't finished it, but there's nothing really there. Even if there is a key . . . or a code."

The two men finished their meal. Suzuki-san ordered garlic ice cream for dessert. Kawamura had another beer.

"I'm going to try the hotel again," said Kawamura sliding out from the restaurant booth, "and Chief Arai's house."

Suzuki-san acknowledged this with another belch.

CHAPTER 34

Noriko Kawamura had always prided herself on being a good driver. She had taken the standard driver's education courses offered after high school, and her father had sent her to a private driving school during her college years as an extra precaution. The results of her tests after these courses were always impressively high. Even her husband, who understood good and bad driving habits as the result of his work, appreciated her talent.

Noriko had organized overnight clothing and supplies and had gotten herself and the children out of the house within a half-hour of her husband's phone call from the tennis club. He probably would have liked it to be quicker, but there were many little details that required attention. As she drove along the busy street, now a rush-hour street, she remembered that she had forgotten her own cosmetics case and her son's clean underwear for tomorrow. But she had agreed with her husband that immediate evacuation of the family in certain circumstances—even if it later proved to be absolutely unnecessary—was an intelligent approach to life in their circumstances. It was one of the burdens of being a police captain's wife.

Tokyo Disneyland was located about forty-five minutes from the city limits—along expressways that eventually merged and went to Narita International Airport. Access roads that led to the expressways were always busy, and the rush-hour traffic just made it worse. Interestingly, a lower percentage of vehicles on the road during rush hour in and around Tokyo were private vehicles. The overwhelming majority were commercial vehicles—trucks and buses—traveling to and from the industrial prefecture of Chiba, northeast of the nation's capital.

Now and then Noriko was able to move the Honda Civic along at the respectable speed of 50 or 60 kilometers per hour, but it was usually just the stop-and-go dance that occurs between stoplights. One hurries, then waits.

Turning left onto the Shuto Expressway #7

entrance ramp offered one of those rare occasions where acceleration and speed made automobile travel seem more reasonable again. Noriko welcomed the tingling of the little bell in the car which warned that she was exceeding 100 kilometers per hour. A sign indicated that Tokyo Disneyland was only 35 kilometers ahead.

To give her credit, no one would have noticed the gray delivery van following the Honda Civic. Not only were the kids arguing in the back seat about the various attractions at Disneyland, there was never really a time when, due to the traffic, she was *not* being followed closely by a vehicle.

Noriko was mildly surprised by the van attempting to overtake her as she merged into the fast-flowing expressway traffic. Her automatic reaction in these situations was not aggressive by any means—she followed her instincts and began to slow down. One lane, her lane, was blending into two lanes, but there were suddenly four vehicles abreast.

The van hit the front right side of the Honda Civic. There was no space. The van did not veer away. The guardposts and cables at the edge of the expressway on the left were dangerously close. Noriko, having been already hit by the van, steered back into it. It was a known entity—the area beyond the guardposts and cables was not.

The van, gray and now huge just outside her window on the right side of the car, continued to push the Honda Civic to the left. Noriko remembered hearing the blare of a horn, then the screeching of ripping metal as the jerks and bumps of the posts and cables indicated that the left side of the car was being torn apart.

The concrete abutment of a bridge was approaching rapidly. Noriko quickly swung the steering wheel away from the van and to the left. The unknown beyond the posts and cables was suddenly preferable. With a heart-stopping jerk, and then the feeling of release as if being catapulted, the Honda Civic crashed beyond the posts and cables. Only the right rear of the car was clipped by the concrete abutment of the bridge. In a suspended moment in time, Noriko wondered if seat belts were fastened. The children were screaming.

The car bounced once on its wheels as it careened down the embankment, but most of the undercarriage was destroyed by the impact. The glancing impact with the concrete abutment had put a slight twist to the flight of humans and machinery. The car bounced again, but at a skewed angle. It flipped over, smashed backwards through a wire fence surrounding a warehouse staging area, and slid on its crushed top across the pavement to a four-meter stack of supplies waiting to be loaded at the dock. A thousand bottles of Calpis—a fermented milk drink favored by Japanese—thundered down onto the Honda Civic.

CHAPTER 35

The origins of the Kempeitai are shrouded in the understandable mists surrounding a nation preparing for war, fighting a war, and then losing a war. Records get lost. And memories of dark days tend to fail.

Some say that the secret police organization had its roots in a Tokyo-based group of dedicated adherents to the Imperial Way during the somewhat turbulent years of change and reformation in the 1920s. Opinions varied in those days as to the direction Japan should take as the country emerged from feudalism and into the middle of twentieth-century world affairs. Assassinations, attempted assassinations, and a myriad of palace and government plots tugged and stretched at the fabric of a society still adapting to modern times.

Several things were clear. Japan had very little in the way of natural resources, industry required resources, and accommodations had to be made. Whether or not those accommodations were made as the result of diplomatic maneuvers, political alliances, or military force were the issues keeping diplomats, politicians, or generals awake into the wee hours.

Japan had astonished everyone by defeating Russia early in the century at a naval battle at the extreme eastern edge of the Asian continent. Subsequent expansion into China and Korea under a passive "open-door" policy maintained by the United States confirmed in the minds of many that acquisition of territory was just one of those rights that the powerful quite naturally held over the weak.

The military gained ascendancy in the 1930s, and the organization that became the Kempeitai owed its allegiance to the national power structure, not just to interested parties in Tokyo.

The role of the secret police became one of gathering internal intelligence, uncovering dissenters, and guaranteeing that the national interests of the power structure were maintained. They were effective, but they were hated and feared by those with independent ideas.

As battles on the Asian continent intensified, the role of the Kempeitai expanded. The conduct of international affairs and the maintenance of standards as defined by the power structure required supervision and control. The flow of refugees back and forth, coupled with a conscripted Japanese military force intermingling with them without the same ideals thoroughly indoctrinated, could result in problems. The Kempeitai took care of those problems.

In many ways, the Kempeitai was the skeleton

upon which the flesh of Japanese aggression hung during the war years between the late 1930s and 1945. There was, of course, fanatic dedication to the Cause at all levels and branches of the military effort—dedicating one's life to Japan and all that that meant—but in case there was a wavering of commitment, the secret police organization was always there to prevent dissension.

At the war's end, Allied forces prosecuted known war criminals. Obvious wrongs were punished by obvious sanctions. Less public organizations tended to fade into the lacquerwork and disappear from scrutiny. For one reason or another, secret medical experiments conducted by Japanese researchers during the war were not brought out into the open. It is today suggested that the Allied powers traded information regarding the findings of those research projects for immunity from prosecution.

The enslavement of thousands to serve as "comfort women" to Japanese troops abroad may have been an issue, but it became an issue relegated to mere sociological and cultural values—not war crimes.

The members of the feared Kempeitai—a shadowy organization to begin with—headed for cover. Some went into police work, some into private business, some became the old men riding bicycles delivering stock certificates in Japan's "Wall Street" district of Marunouchi. None made public their activities during the war effort. As years went by, it was far better to have served as a ground soldier in any of the theaters of war, or to have sailed a ship or flown a plane, than to have been a member of the secret police. Running a car off the road to Disneyland would have been child's play to them.

CHAPTER 36

"I can't believe it would take so long to get there," said Kawamura to Suzuki-san. The two men were on the train to Kawamura's neighborhood.

"Rush hour?" suggested Suzuki-san.

"Maybe," said Kawamura. "But it's been almost three hours. My wife would have gotten the kids out of the house and on the road pretty quickly. They should have been at the hotel an hour ago."

"Did you have enough gas in the car?" asked Suzuki-san.

"Probably not," answered Kawamura. "That car never has enough gas. That could be the problem. You don't mind coming with me?"

"Not at all," said Suzuki-san. "I'm fluid, but I think you're worrying too much. "I'm more interested in hearing what those memoirs have to say."

The train stopped at stations Kawamura usually slept through.

"The memoirs seem to be entering Manabe-san's semiretirement and the tennis phase. Tennis is boring to begin with, and reading about it is even worse." Kawamura was a baseball player.

Kawamura and Suzuki-san quickly walked along the narrow lanes from the train station to the Kawamura residence. There were still many straggling commuters on their way home, and most of the shops were still open and doing a flourishing business in fast food, flowers, or liquor. No one, either in Kawamura's house or at Chief Arai's home, had answered Kawamura's phone calls from the subway station.

"The only place she'll know where to reach me, if she has any trouble, is at home," said Kawamura.

"You do realize," said Suzuki-san struggling to keep up and sweating profusely in the process, "that all the events could have been what they appeared to be?"

"Your namesake Suzuki falling down the stairs in his own place and breaking his neck?"

"It could have happened."

"Arai hanging himself in his own kitchen?"

"It could have happened."

"Shig Manabe?"

Suzuki-san didn't answer. He was wiping his head with a bright red handkerchief.

"By the way," continued Kawamura, "what did you do with the original disk that you found in Manabe-san's machine? Someone seems to want that very much."

"Don't worry. It's in the mail," said Suzuki-san.

"In the mail?"

"To, ah, my wife. By the time she forwards it on

to the other . . . you know, and then *she* forwards
it to the next . . . "

"I understand."

" . . . it will be revolving around in the postal
system for the next three weeks."

Kawamura and Suzuki-san turned onto the
short walkway leading to the front of a three-floor
apartment building. Automobiles in the Honda
Civic category were parked on either side of the
walkway—economics and the lack of space guar-
anteed that large foreign cars were never in sight.

Kawamura brushed past a number of bicycles
in the lobby, ignored the elevator, and went up to
the second floor two steps at a time. Suzuki-san
followed, noting to himself that Kawamura never
took stairs when an elevator was present.

Kawamura paused at one of the three apartment entrances on the second floor and fumbled
with his keys.

"Take it easy," said Suzuki-san. Kawamura was
obviously stressed.

The door opened easily, and Kawamura looked
puzzled.

"Was that door locked?" asked Kawamura, almost to himself.

"It probably was," said Suzuki-san, "but you
should have tried it first."

"Even if she was in a hurry, my wife would have
locked the door," said Kawamura frowning. "But
it's too late to know now."

Suzuki-san followed Kawamura into the apartment. To his eye, the place seemed to be reason-

ably neat with most things in their proper places. To Kawamura's eye, the apartment was the scene of more chaos than Noriko would normally permit. A suitcase, obviously discarded in the packing process, lay on the floor with only his wife's cosmetics case and his son's underwear in it. Closet doors, usually shut, hung open revealing the mass of clothing required of an active family of four. Several empty clothes hangers lay on the floor.

"Well, they got out of here," said Kawamura, "and obviously in a hurry."

"Is anything out of place?" asked Suzuki-san, standing in his stockinged feet on one of Noriko's T-shirts.

Kawamura realized that his wife had always cleaned the house before he came home at night.

"I can't really tell," said Kawamura. "Let's hope she calls."

Kawamura walked into the bedroom used by his daughter. That room always tended to be a mess. Despite his wife's efforts, Kawamura's daughter seemed to prefer dwelling in what could only be described as the aftermath of a typhoon.

Kawamura's son was marginally neater. Kawamura stood in the doorway of that room and looked at the treasures of a young teenage boy. As the pattern of things in the room became clear, Kawamura noticed it.

The computer game equipment, none of which Kawamura understood, was on its usual table, but was facing front to the wall. On the floor were the greatest treasures of the young teenager. The peculiar little diskettes containing the electronic framework for the games were out of their plastic cases—some of which had been broken in haste—and were scattered about the floor in mind-numbing randomness. *That* was something his son would never do. He always kept everything to do with his computer scrupulously neat and tidy.

Kawamura began to yell for Suzuki-san when the phone rang.

"I'll get it," said Suzuki-san who was already in the kitchen looking for something to eat and standing next to the phone.

"Is it Noriko?" asked Kawamura walking through the living-dining area.

Suzuki-san turned and looked at Kawamura, his normally red face, and head, were white.

"Yes, I understand. Yes, he's here. Yes, we can find it," Suzuki-san was saying into the phone. "Yes, I'll tell him, and I'll call right back. See what else you can get."

Suzuki-san hung up before Kawamura could take the receiver from his hand.

"Noriko?"

"Let's sit down," said Suzuki-san.

"No. Who was on the phone?"

Suzuki-san pushed past Kawamura and went to the living room and sat at the low table. Kawamura followed, then sat.

"That was one of the night duty staff at the Azabu Station. They traced the registration of the car to you at the station."

"What car?" Kawamura was almost screaming. He did not like the look on his assistant's face.

"Your car," answered Suzuki-san carefully. "There's been an accident. Everyone is still alive, but it doesn't look good."

CHAPTER 37

Kawamura pounded on the steering wheel in frustration. He had borrowed the car from his neighbor downstairs, and he was now fighting his way through post-rush-hour traffic which would remain heavy until at least midnight. Kawamura knew the hospital in Chiba; it was where his father-in-law had died three years before.

Suzuki-san, with some reluctance, had remained at the apartment. Kawamura had ordered a complete search of his residence by the Azabu Police Station experts. It was standard procedure whenever an officer's home was broken into. Suzuki-san was also given the phone numbers of Kawamura's mother-in-law and sister-in-law. Noriko's mother had a bad heart, and Suzuki-san's surprisingly sensitive way of explaining things would be preferable to having the old lady hear about her daughter's accident on the news. That would probably kill her.

The information from the hospital was sketchy. All anyone would tell him over the phone was that all three people were in critical condition. It was, Kawamura was told, too early to make a firm diagnosis, but it appeared that his wife might have broken her neck, "but we don't know if the paralysis is permanent." The children, who had been in the back seat, had also suffered broken bones, and one of them, Kawamura was not certain which, had lost a great deal of blood.

As Kawamura finally roared onto the express-way, he hoped he would meet a patrol car. It would at least be able to lead him with sirens and lights to the hospital.

The worse thing, Kawamura realized, was that this whole thing was *his* fault. If he had not overreacted, the family members would be in their own beds, not hospital beds. Maybe, just maybe, someone had waited outside his apartment look-ing for an opportunity to search it, but that threat was now less serious than the current reality. Traffic in and around Tokyo was getting worse every year—a truck suddenly cut in front of Kawamura—and sending the family out into that traffic at night was unpardonable. Kawamura thought of his loved ones lying ahead in a hospi-tal, and began to cry. He rolled down the window and reached over to the briefcase containing the memoirs. He almost threw the whole thing out the window, but an airport bus charging up from the rear caused him to redirect his focus on driving.

Kawamura pulled into the Chiba hospital parking lot and parked his neighbor's car in a Doctors Only space. It was almost 10:00 P.M., and no one in authority seemed to be concerned with whether or not an outsider should be walking around looking for information. The guard in the guard booth did not even look up as Kawamura charged past. A patient, in pajamas and smoking a cigarette, directed Kawamura to the third floor.

Kawamura ran into Noriko's sister and her husband outside the nurse's station. They lived in Chiba and had responded to Suzuki-san's call immediately. The sister was in tears, her husband was in his cups.

"This is terrible," reported the sister.

"This is inconvenient," slurred the brother-in-law.

"Who's in charge here?" asked Kawamura, accustomed to bureaucracy.

A senior nurse in her mid-forties and a doctor in his early twenties eventually emerged from a cul-de-sac behind the nurses' station. Beyond the gray cloth covering the entrance to the cul-de-sac, Kawamura caught a glimpse of a kettle steaming on a hot plate.

"You are the husband and the father?" asked the young doctor, almost accusingly.

"Yes," responded Kawamura. "I am Captain Kawamura of the Azabu Police Station, and I demand to know the condition of the patients."

The condition, as it turned out, was not good. Noriko had suffered massive injuries in the head and neck areas, and the extent of her injuries could not be confirmed until the senior doctors arrived the first thing in the morning.

Kawamura's son had most probably broken his right arm and collar bone, but he was conscious and already complaining about things.

Kawamura's daughter had more serious injuries. Nothing seemed to be broken, but she was hemorrhaging internally, and as a result had gone into and out of shock several times since being brought to the hospital.

The next hour was a blur to Kawamura. He donated blood once for his daughter, held his wife Noriko's hand for two or three minutes, and talked briefly with his son. His sister-in-law also donated blood, but her husband's blood was determined to have an alcohol content beyond the acceptable range.

By midnight it became obvious that nothing more would develop until the morning. The sister-in-law and the brother-in-law left—the brother-in-law, a clerk in the electronics discount area of Akihabara, mumbled something about bringing TV sets back with him the next day.

Kawamura sat on the ragged couch outside the third-floor rooms. A coffee machine hummed and clanked around the corner. The general wisdom in Japan was that the best hospitals had the most primitive physical facilities. Kawamura hoped that was true. The place was primitive, and more staff members than he could imagine being on duty streamed out of the facility as the minutes wore by. Those were *his* family members in there fighting for their lives, and everyone seemed to be going home.

Kawamura called his apartment, talked to Suzuki-san, and learned that nothing was new. The Azabu Police Department technicians had been through the premises, but no reports were imminent until all the details were carefully scrutinized.

"Did your son smoke?" asked Suzuki-san at one point.

"Of course not, er, I don't think so. Why?"

"Our people found evidence of cigarette ash on the floor in his room," said Suzuki-san.

"That's all?" asked Kawamura.

"That's all," confirmed Suzuki-san. "At least for now."

"Have you contacted Chief Arai yet?" asked Kawamura.

"No one answers," replied Suzuki-san. "And our people are worried about that."

"Keep trying," instructed Kawamura. "I'm staying here at the hospital."

"By the way," said Suzuki-san before he hung up. "Your neighbor downstairs wants to know when you plan to return his car."

"Tell him to get stuffed," said Kawamura quite simply.

Kawamura paced back and forth for a few moments after hanging up. He looked at his briefcase containing the memoirs lying on the ragged couch. He wished he had never heard of the Tokyo Lawn Tennis Club or Shig Manabe.

He finally decided to call the police station in Chiba. It wouldn't help, but Kawamura wanted to know the details of the accident. He was told that out of professional courtesy the investigating officers, who were still on duty, would go to the hospital as soon as they had a chance and give him their report.

Kawamura paced back and forth some more, tried to go into the rooms containing his wife, son, and daughter, was told that was inadvisable, and went back to the ragged couch. He picked up the damned manuscript and continued reading.

> In looking back on everything, the most amazing thing to me has been the wide range of people encountered throughout the different stages of my life. There have been genuine heroes, and genuine villains. There have been people of strength, honesty, and dignity, there have been people who were weak and without principles. Most helped me up, but some pushed until I almost collapsed.

Shig Manabe was obviously beginning to wrap up the story of his life. And his way of doing it seemed to be one of taking the last people he had encountered and summarizing his relationships with them first. To Kawamura's way of thinking, it was just one more maddening aspect of Manabe-san's approach.

> Dr. Edith Barker was one of the more remarkable individuals I ever met. She was warm, caring, and a selfless and able administrator.

Knowing that I had an interest in orphans, illegitimate children, and youngsters from broken homes, she was the one who got me involved with the New York Home for Foundling Children

Right, thought Kawamura to himself, and I wonder how many of those children he had fathered.

On the other hand, Aaron Jorgenson—a fellow director at the Home—was one of most despicable individuals I ever met. His arrest and conviction for abusing *his own children* created a scandal that nearly closed the place.

Whether or not Dr. Edith Barker and Aaron Jorgenson were real names, those people's activities probably had nothing to do with the current situation in Tokyo. Manabe-san had described Jorgenson as being grossly overweight, and that did not fit any of the foreigners at the tennis club. Abusing one's own children *was* terrible, however, and *he* should have been killed in the bath.

Kawamura stood up and went to his daughter's room. The nurse on duty still advised against a visit, but Kawamura demanded that he be allowed to at least see her again.

His daughter was semiconscious. Kawamura held his hand to her forehead, looked up at the blood that was being continually dripped into her veins, and fought the urge to cry.

He left the room and visited his son. He had been placed in a ward containing grown men. A nurse, her back to the door, was adjusting something near the bed of a man at the far wall. Kawamura looked down at his son's bed. He had been heavily sedated, and his entire upper torso was wrapped in bandages.

"He should be all right," said the nurse softly. She had floated soundlessly over to Kawamura's elbow.

"How do you know?" he asked.

"Because he's young," said the nurse. "And you should leave the room."

Kawamura walked into his wife's room. A nurse and the young doctor were watching dials monitoring her vital signs.

"You should not . . . ," began the doctor, protesting.

"I know," interrupted Kawamura.

He walked over to the bed were Noriko lay with her head bound, the bindings firmly attached to the sides of the bed. Her arms were strapped to her waist. Her eyes seemed to have blackened even more during the last hour. Kawamura leaned down and kissed her on the nose, then left the room. More than anything, he wanted to scream.

CHAPTER 38

A police officer from Chiba was standing by the ragged couch as Kawamura emerged from his wife's room.

"Captain Kawamura?"

"Yes, thank you for coming."

The police officer looked around, obviously uncomfortable in hospital surroundings.

"Your car?" asked Kawamura.

"Yes," said the policeman, relieved.

Kawamura joined the policeman and his Chiba partner in the squad car parked in the emergency entrance.

"No doubt about it," said the first policeman. "It was hit-and-run. But an airport bus driver got the license number. Unmarked Toyota delivery van, reported stolen in Tokyo yesterday. We'll find it."

Kawamura was shocked.

"You're certain?"

"We're certain he didn't stop. And from the bus driver's description of what he saw, that van deliberately steered into your wife's car. He didn't have to. The bus and a truck both slowed down. The van had plenty of room."

Kawamura looked out the window of the squad car. This was unbelievable. Or was it?

"Description of driver or passengers?"

"Too dark," said the policeman. But the bus driver thinks there was no passenger. Of course in vans you can't always see."

The three men sat in silence. The police radio called reports and numbers in the background.

"Any connection with something you're working on?" asked the driver of the squad car.

Kawamura paused before answering.

"I don't know," he finally said. "I thought this . . . thing was an accident. Now I don't know."

"It looks serious," said the policeman.

"I'm afraid it is," said Kawamura. "Do me a favor and get the report to the Azabu Police Station as soon as possible."

"We'll fax it out before we go home tonight," said the policeman. "Is there anyplace we can take you?"

"No, thank you," answered Kawamura getting out of the car. "I'll stay here tonight."

"How are they?" asked the policeman.

"Too early to tell," said Kawamura.

"Good luck," said the driver starting the engine. "Oh, by the way. Do you like Calpis?"

"Calpis?" repeated Kawamura. "I hate the stuff. Why?"

"You may want to start drinking it," said the driver. "Your car hit crates of it stacked by the warehouse dock. The bottles broke and splashed all over the area. That's probably why there wasn't an explosion and fire."

"I still hate the stuff," said Kawamura shaking his head and walking back into the hospital.

CHAPTER 39

Kawamura called his house and there was no answer. Suzuki-san had obviously gone off to wherever "home" was that month. He then called Chief Arai's house—noting that it was 3:00 in the morning—and there was no answer. Kawamura finally called the Azabu Police Station.

The night desk officer had no idea where Chief Arai was—in fact, he explained, he had never even *met* Chief Arai. He *did* know, based on a memo he had just received, that a Chief Matsubara was the temporary acting chief of the Azabu Station. The night desk officer had never met Chief Matsubara either.

Kawamura reported the details as he knew them of his wife's accident, including a summary of his discussion with the Chiba policemen. Again, it was part of standard operating procedure whenever officers or families were involved in anything that could be considered suspicious.

"Didn't we just send a forensics team to your house?" asked the desk officer.

"Yes," answered Kawamura.

"And you're in a hospital in Chiba with your family?"

"Yes," answered Kawamura.

"Is this connected with a case you're working on?"

Kawamura could visualize the night desk officer carefully writing everything down.

"I have no idea," answered Kawamura. "I'm on vacation." Kawamura could not imagine a leak in his station, but until he could get in touch with Chief Arai, he decided to err on the side of caution.

"Well, you don't seem to be having a good vacation."

"That's a fact," said Kawamura, hanging up the phone. He and the night desk officer had never met either.

Kawamura visited each of his family members again—getting in trouble each time—then returned to the ragged couch and the memoirs with a cup of burnt coffee from the machine. The frustration was almost overwhelming—clearly everything was connected to the murder at the tennis club—but there was really nothing he could do. At least, by remaining at the hospital, he was protecting his family.

Manabe-san's summary continued backwards through the years. He had gotten involved with the American Heart Association because of the death of his New York office landlord who had cardiac arrest at the age of forty-nine. Manabe had once been invited to the White House as the result of his efforts, and was very proud of his picture taken with President Gerald Ford.

President Ford asked me if I liked to play golf. I told him no, I have never played golf. He laughed and laughed over that, then told the photographers he wanted one more picture with the Japanese gentleman who never played golf. We all laughed about that afterwards.

In his role as a fund-raiser for the Republican Party, Manabe-san got close to New York City Mayor John Lindsay.

Mayor Lindsay gave us the same kind of enthusiasm we had developed for President Kennedy. I thought Mayor Lindsay was a brilliant man, even a charismatic leader, but he eventually got tired of the problems in the city and went back to private practice.

Kawamura vaguely remembered the name Lindsay and concluded it had nothing to do with the murder at the tennis club.

Going back through the years, Manabe-san seemed to be summarizing his impressions of the people passing through his life. There was a "hateful bastard" who cheated him out of payment for a consignment of pearls, there was a "beloved man" who came to his rescue once when Communist witch hunts were sweeping the country. The Dean of the Liberal Arts College at the University of Michigan took him in when he ran out of money, and fed and housed him for a complete semester.

Throughout it all, Manabe-san appeared to be very honest about things, if not slightly emotional, but there was still the irritating tendency to mix real with made-up names. Kawamura recognized President Ford's name, and maybe John Lindsay's name, but he had no idea who the hell the Dean of the Liberal Arts College at the University of Michigan was. And there was still the situation where Kawamura *knew* who the real people were. Referring to Theodore Bitman, the Mormon missionary, pearl dealer, and Japanese TV talent, Manabe-san's remarks were as follows:

> Tom Backman always struck me as being insincere. Of course I appreciated his commitment to living in Japan as a foreigner—I had made the same commitment to living in America as a foreigner—but I advanced him the money to start his business as an experiment. For all I know, people had been nice to me as an experiment. And did I have anything to demonstrate trustworthiness to them? Probably not. The worst thing about the Backman affair is that he and I verbally agreed that all exports would go through me. Did I have it in writing? No, but I was brought up to trust a person's word. It embarrassed me in front of my wife and her family, but I guess we live and learn. The settlement says that we get ten percent of his net profits. Was that a good deal for us? Yes, it was, a very good deal. Did we actually get ten percent of his profits? I'd be surprised if we get

three or four percent of his profits. As I said before, we live and learn.

Kawamura got up from the ragged couch and went looking for the stern lady who seemed to be the head nurse on the floor. He found her asleep at the desk next to the elevator.

"Your family is OK," said the head nurse when Kawamura woke her. "If not," she added in an accent not unlike Chief Arai's, "this thing would send an alarm." She pointed to a gray box with dials which looked like something out of an early Godzilla movie.

Kawamura went out and walked around the parking lot, always keeping his eye on the front entrance of the hospital. He did deep knee-bends with his hand on the front fender of a 1971 Nissan Fairlady badly in need of a wash, until he realized there were probably other entrances to the hospital. He hurried back to the third floor, checked— under protest—with the family, and returned to the ragged couch.

Manabe-san had unaccountably skipped back in time to his years as a young boy in Seattle. It was as if the war years never existed.

The worst thing was when they called me a "Chinaman." A boy named Walter Brunowski, who had only been in the United States one year longer than me, hit me with a cement block on the playground. Some of the other kids kicked me when I was on the ground. If Speed McCoy hadn't come to my rescue, I might never have lived through that day. I always avoided Walter Brunowski whenever I saw him in the corridors, but he once got me in the locker room. He forced me to eat a bar of soap. I told my father about it when I got home that night, and he told me to always say I was Japanese and to be proud of it. I was sick for a week after that, but when I returned to school, Speed started teaching me how to play baseball. Walter Brunowski was eventually sent to a reform school.

Manabe-san recounted the happy times in Seattle. His successes in baseball predominated, but there were surprisingly little things that made an impression on the youngster.

On warm evenings in the summertime, we would get in the car and go up to the main street in the shopping area near my house. My father would go into Nihan and Martin's drugstore and buy ice cream cones. My mother, father and I would sit in the car and eat the ice cream. Outside, on the sidewalk and leaning against other cars, would be what seemed like hundreds of high school kids lounging around and teasing each other. It all seemed so natural, and now as I think back on it, so innocent. Everyone seemed to be happy and having so much fun. I began to recognize my favorite guys, and I wanted to be like them when I grew up.

There was a bowling alley on the same street—Simon's Bowling Alley—and once in a while my father would take my mother and me into it. We would sit quietly in the back and watch the people bowl. The people were enjoying themselves, and sometimes they would talk to us. My mother did not speak English very well, and so I would always answer when they asked her questions. It was 1939 in America, and in many ways it was the happiest time of my life. I wanted to be a bowling alley pin-setter when I grew up.

Kawamura leaned back on the ragged couch and thought about his own grade-school days. His father had died in the war—at Guam—but his mother used to take him out on warm summer evenings, more than a decade later, to where the fishermen would return from a day on the sea. People would sit around, argue good-naturedly about their catches, and make grandiose plans for the next day. Kawamura could still remember the smells and sounds, and in many ways *they* were the happiest times of his life. Somewhat reluctantly, Kawamura began to appreciate the things that went on in Manabe-san's mind.

Kawamura rose from the ragged couch and walked to the window. It had not been his imagination: it was beginning to get light. Beyond the gray concrete buildings and elevated highways, the sky in the east was preparing for the rising sun.

Kawamura returned to the couch and the memoirs. The final chapter, and perhaps the longest chapter, was reserved for the war years. Shig Manabe's organization was a little peculiar, but his intention was not. Had Kawamura begun at the end of the manuscript, he would have known

that the murder at the Tokyo Lawn Tennis Club
had not yet occurred.

CHAPTER 40

They were worse than the most savage animals. I think about them every day of my life.
For many years I regretted I did nothing to stop
them. It gave me nightmares almost every night.
As time went by, I realized that I could not have
done anything at the time, except get myself
killed.

Shig Manabe was talking about the Kempeitai.

They would deliberately set up our own
people—make traps for them by pretending to
be understanding about the difficulties we were
all undergoing. If anyone was foolish enough to
agree that things were not going well, and there
were a number of innocent young men who did
that, then the Kempeitai would take them away
and execute them.

Manabe went on to explain that things were
even worse for non-Japanese who ran afoul of the
Kempeitai.

They found a young Chinese boy, maybe
twelve or thirteen, walking along by the side of
the railroad tracks near our camp. When they

questioned him, the young boy was so nervous he began to speak some language that sounded like Russian. He had some rice and pickled vegetables in his backpack and our Army people took it. But the Army guards let him go after they took his food. The Kempeitai commander ordered the boy to return. The guards brought the boy back, and the commander—in front of all of us—put his gun to the boy's head and shot him. He then made us cut up the boy, boil his flesh, and serve a "banquet" to our prisoners. We did it. The boy could have been a spy, we were told.

Speed McCoy, Manabe's hero, was in the camp at the time. The Kempeitai commander was the hated Moto who later shot Manabe in the foot. When it was discovered that Manabe was giving Speed *his* food instead, Moto forced Manabe to eat parts of the dead boy. Manabe did.

The Kempeitai officers had quotas, and to demonstrate that they were doing their jobs, they had to uncover traitors. We were just a group of translators—we weren't high enough in any organization to be considered traitors—but those were the circumstances we were in. Actually, I think they were jealous of us because we could speak the language of our prisoners. My friend Miyabe, who I later hired as my first employee, was caught by Moto laughing with one of the prisoners. Moto castrated Miyabe. I found him years later in a hospital near Tokyo. Miyabe never fought back, but I have decided to fight back now.

Kawamura put the memoirs on the ragged couch and leaned his head back. "Miyabe"—in Manabe's bizarre way of disguising names—was Kimura, the man with the cravat and paisley shirt. Kimura had fought with Manabe on one of the tennis courts, refused later to play even on the next court, and is closing out his years stacking books in a Japanese-American publishing company.

> Moto hated Americans more than any other people. That was the most difficult thing for me because of my background. I did not hate Americans *or* Japanese. But I hated Moto.
> Moto used to say that Americans were the reason Japan was being persecuted. If America had not blocked trade of essential materials Japan needed from Southeast Asia, there would not be the current problem.
> To demonstrate his hatred, Moto refused to give Speed more food. I can never be absolutely certain about that, or if Speed would have lived anyway, but I do know about another case. We had a new prisoner in camp named Brennan. The only thing I remember about him is that he was from a place called Oil City, Pennsylvania. He was basically healthy, but one night he was vomiting. Moto kicked him in the head many times. He said only Americans vomit like dogs. Brennan stopped vomiting. He was dead.

Kawamura had difficulty adjusting to Manabe's tone in this last chapter. Until now Manabe had recounted his adventures without any sign of real passion or feeling. Most people—Japanese or American—were very nice. A few were boneheads.

But this was different. Manabe was setting the stage by describing his background, his passive or active relationships, and his general outlook on life. Illegitimate children had no place in the memoirs. Reports of business successes or problems, along with other events in the man's life, were nothing more than techniques for establishing credentials.

> The day we surrendered was one I'll never forget. Of course I was in pain because of the bullet wound in my foot. But when Moto began screaming about American devils and our responsibility to fight to the end, I thought we all would be killed. Moto shot one of our translators and our Army captain. The Americans may have opened fire, but one of our people—I don't even know who—hit him in the face with his rifle butt. That's probably why I didn't recognize him at first when I met him years later. Moto's face had been fixed. But I'll never forget that pink scar on the back of his neck. It's the last thing I saw before I passed out.

Kawamura could not remember a pink scar on anyone's neck, but he hadn't been looking for one. In any event, Manabe's memoirs continued with a ghoulish totaling of people he had seen Moto kill. It was an insane mixture of war prisoners and fellow-Japanese. Moto had even contrived to have rats attack an American who refused to admit that President Truman was a devil. Thankfully,

Manabe did not go into details, but the American was blinded by the experience.

> And now to think that he is an "honored and respected" man. It is even rumored that he will soon receive an Imperial award for his contribution to international understanding. He does not know who I am—I was just dirt at the time to him—but now the truth must be revealed. I'm probably the only one left who remembers.

Manabe's serpentine method of mixing real and made-up names was probably not important. It was, Kawamura realized, perhaps the man's way of protecting the innocent. If there was a key to any of this, it would be one used only to confirm the basic truth of the memoirs.

What Shig Manabe had done with his memoirs was to bring down, and essentially kill, his vision of pure evil. Former Ambassador to the United States, and current Tokyo Lawn Tennis Club president, Tatsuo Morimoto was the target.

CHAPTER 41

Suzuki-san entered the waiting room just as sunlight was beginning to stream in the window. Kawamura, on the ragged couch, was lightly dozing—haunting visions of starving prisoners of war, starving captors, mud, rats, fear, and all the related insanities of humans at war swirling in his exhausted mind.

"How are they?" asked Suzuki-san. He was wearing his blue suit and carrying a shopping bag.

"Ah, we'll know better in an hour," said Kawamura looking at his watch. "The senior doctor will look at them then."

Kawamura stood up and stretched. Suzuki-san opened the shopping bag and spread fried rice cakes wrapped in plastic on the couch. He also pulled two cans of hot tea from the bag. Early-morning hospital workers were beginning to shuffle back and forth in greater numbers.

"Where are your neighbor's car keys?" asked Suzuki-san. "I checked out a pool car from the station, and my wife can drive the other one back."

Suzuki-san took the keys and left. Kawamura walked to the window and watched Suzuki-san handing the keys in the parking lot to a woman Kawamura had never seen before. It was a lifestyle he could never understand, Kawamura realized as he turned and walked down the corridor to Noriko's room.

The condition of the family members was still not clear. The arriving day staff would only state that vital signs seemed to have stabilized since the accident, but the doctors would know better.

Kawamura returned to the ragged couch.

Suzuki-san was seated comfortably eating a rice cake.

"Anything from Shig Manabe's memoirs?" asked Suzuki-san.

Kawamura sat next to his partner and opened a can of tea.

"Everything is in the memoirs," said Kawamura. "And for the first time, I *really* don't know what to do."

"Eat," advised Suzuki-san. "Then talk."

Kawamura took a bite of the cake. And then talked.

It seemed clearer to him as he verbalized his thoughts. Suzuki-san sat patiently and listened, interrupting only occasionally.

"But the keys were only important in case someone wanted to corroborate background details or facts," explained Kawamura. "Shig Manabe probably didn't want to hurt his first employee, Kimura, or Theodore Bitman for that matter. In fact *all* the names, except President Ford, Mayor Lindsay, and Sakai, could have been disguised. It isn't important to the main thrust of his work. He wanted to bring down Moto, the Kempeitai man who became ambassador to the United States."

"Still, the name Moto . . . "

"In *that* case, Moto may have been the man's real name. He changed identities and background right after the war—something that may have been easy to do then—and embarked on his career as Morimoto. Even if he didn't change his name, one punch of the keyboard would change the name Moto to Morimoto in Manabe's manuscript. Maybe Shig Manabe *was* being obsessively careful until the publication date."

A middle-aged doctor approached Kawamura. Kawamura followed him into his tiny office. X-rays were clipped along a light on the wall. They were pictures of the insides of Kawamura's loved ones.

"We plan to drill two holes in your wife's skull," said the doctor, "to prevent brain damage from the swelling."

Kawamura heard the words, but it was all he could do to keep from swinging out at something—anything.

"And," continued the doctor, "then we'll be able to move her into a better position to determine the extent of injuries to her neck and spine."

"Will she be able to . . . ?"

"We don't know yet if the paralysis is permanent," said the doctor, anticipating and answering the question. "Your son's condition is more certain. He broke these bones here," continued the doctor pointing to the two middle X-rays, "and they can be fixed."

Kawamura stared through a field of vision narrowed by panic at incomprehensible gray-and-black shadows on the film.

"Which bones?" asked Kawamura.

"Ones inside his body," replied the doctor in a tone commonly used when explaining mysteries of the human machine to unknowing laymen. "His arm, his collar bone, and the clavicle."

Kawamura stared at the gray-and-black shadows.

"And my daughter?"

The doctor took down the X-rays and put up four more.

"Your daughter's condition is still not clear. She probably has a serious concussion, but she is also bleeding internally. That could be caused by this."

The doctor pointed to the right side of an obvious rib cage. Three ribs were clearly broken.

"We will monitor her condition this morning. If the bleeding does not slow down, we will do exploratory surgery."

"Baka!" yelled Kawamura as he tried to rise from the chair in the doctor's tiny office. He was suddenly dizzy, and even more suddenly he was seated again in the chair. He may have lost touch with things for a moment. The doctor already had a glass of water in his hand, and somehow a nurse had entered the room.

"Take this," said the doctor handing Kawamura two pills.

Kawamura pushed the pills away.

"I understand you're a police officer," said the doctor.

"Yes, one who nearly killed his family."

"Listen to me. You and I are both professionals. There is nothing you can do now. You should understand that. Go get some rest. I promise we will do our best for your family."

Kawamura drank the water, got up, and walked slowly back to the waiting room. He had never felt more frustrated in his life.

Suzuki-san rose from the ragged couch as Kawamura returned.

"Are they OK?"

"No, they're not," said Kawamura, "and there's nothing I can do about it."

"Are you OK?"

"Am I OK? How the hell can I be OK?" snapped Kawamura. "My wife may be . . . "

Kawamura stopped and put his hand on his assistant's shoulder.

"Sorry, my friend. I feel so helpless. That bastard Morimoto, or whatever his name is, is behind this. I wish I could get to Chief Arai. Maybe . . . "

"Let's go then," said Suzuki-san picking up paper and the remains of the rice cake.

"But where the hell is he?"

"He called your house last night after you left. Actually it was early this morning. I spoke to him. I said I'd arrange a meeting."

"Why didn't you tell me?" asked Kawamura.

"You," said Suzuki-san looking around the hospital waiting room, "had other things on your mind."

Kawamura followed Suzuki-san down a flight of stairs, then to a service elevator at the rear of the hospital building.

"You parked down here?"

"Not exactly," answered Suzuki-san. "The pool

car from the station is still in the main parking lot, along with six people from our station."

"Six people from our station?"

"Actually," said Suzuki-san as they entered an underground garage, "they are sort of off-duty. It's not a good time for your family to receive . . . ah . . . visitors, and they'll spread around and make sure of that."

Suzuki-san nodded at a young man Kawamura vaguely recognized from the station, then walked up to a battered old Toyota covered with equal parts of rust and dirt.

"Where's *this* car from?"

"Your friends from the Chiba Police Station dropped this off for us. Unofficially, of course. We shouldn't have anyone follow us."

"Where are we meeting Chief Arai?" asked Kawamura as he got into the passenger seat.

"Disneyland," answered Suzuki-san.

CHAPTER 42

Kawamura, with a day's growth of beard, Suzuki, in his blue serge suit, and Chief Arai, in a multi-colored Hawaiian shirt and white trousers, sat at a picnic table. Disney's Magic Mountain loomed in the distance. In the background, a Mississippi riverboat bumped and bobbed through a man-made canal cut into what was probably a farmer's rice paddy only months before.

They were joined by Captain Ogishi of the Ueno Police Station who, clearly off-duty, was visiting the theme park with his family. He was wearing jeans, a T-shirt bearing the inscription "Eat Trees for the Love of Human," and dark glasses. An older man, who was introduced as Chief Arai's counterpart at the Shirogane Police Station where Suzuki the yakitori man had his establishment, was there along with the driver of the police car from the Chiba Police Station. The driver, seen once before in uniform, was wearing a ballooning shirt straight from the reruns of "Miami Vice."

"His neck was broken," reported the older man from the Shirogane Station, "but it says here that he also suffered intermediate hemorrhaging from a blow to his stomach shortly before his death." The Shirogane man was reading from a preliminary autopsy report describing the death of the landlord of Shig Manabe's hole.

"That's similar to our report on Sakai," said Captain Ogishi from Ueno.

"What about the, ah, accident on the expressway?" asked Chief Arai. Out of sheer force of personality, he now led the "unofficial" meeting.

"In our . . . opinion, the delivery van deliberately drove Captain Kawamura's car off the road. Drunken or sleeping drivers tend to overreact in the opposite direction whenever a collision is imminent. According to our witness, an airport bus driver, the van did not overreact . . . in fact the driver of the van seemed to rather skillfully nudge the car off the road."

Kawamura sat in a trance. Young families, innocently romping back and forth along the walkway, were worlds apart from his concerns.

"And," continued the man from Chiba in the billowing shirt, "we finally found the vehicle. In the parking lot of the Hilton Hotel next door."

"Anything . . .?" asked Suzuki-san.

"No," answered the man from Chiba. "It was clean."

The officers of the law—Hawaiian shirt, blue serge suit, T-shirt, sedate business suits, and a Don Johnson "hip" thing—looked at each other.

"What do you have?" Chief Arai asked Kawamura.

Kawamura described Shig Manabe's memoirs. The first seventy-five percent was devoted to Manabe-san's interesting but somewhat mundane life. The last part was a scathing revelation of the activities of the Kempeitai during the war and specifically the activities of an animal now exalted in international circles.

"He said," reported Kawamura, "that he was probably signing his death warrant by publicizing the story, but he said he owed it to future generations." Kawamura did not go into a discussion of keys.

The officers of the law sat for a moment in silence. A young family with two children came up and sat at the end of the picnic table and began to unwrap packages of food from home smuggled into the Disney complex. The children had Mickey Mouse balloons. Chief Arai barked something to them—Kawamura didn't hear what—and the young family got up immediately and left.

"The Kempeitai are dying," said Chief Arai at last, "but their influence still exists."

The older man from the Shirogane Police Station nodded in agreement.

"Some joined the police department," said Chief Arai, "and some have risen to positions of power. We still have to deal with them."

"Why do we have to deal with those bastards?" asked Kawamura suddenly. "If they *were* criminals, they still *are* criminals."

"What's a criminal?" asked Chief Arai, leaning forward in his Hawaiian shirt. "They were patriots in their day . . . superpatriots. We can't ignore that."

"Ignore it?" said Kawamura rising from the picnic bench. "You're as bad as they are. They killed . . . "

Suzuki-san put his arm on Kawamura's shoulder and pulled him down.

"Look, Kawamura-kun," said Chief Arai, "I feel worse than anybody about your wife and children. I should have *forced* you away from this. But at the time I didn't know what was behind it all. We still don't have proof of anything."

"Shig Manabe's memoirs . . . "

"Shig Manabe's memoirs," interrupted Chief Arai, "just tell us that someone who may or may not be your friend Ambassador Morimoto was a particularly hated Kempeitai man. He's probably one of thousands."

"But the other ones didn't later become ambassadors to the United States," said Kawamura.

"All right, I'll grant you that Morimoto had a very strong interest in keeping his past secret," said Chief Arai. "I'll even grant you that it may have been a motive for murder—particularly for one who seems so taken with himself—but we still don't have proof of anything."

The policemen sat at the picnic table looking decidedly gloomy by comparison to their surroundings.

"There had to be more than one person," said Captain Ogishi from Ueno. "Whoever Morimoto was, I don't think he could have picked up Sakai and hanged him."

"And Suzuki from the yakitori restaurant was a pretty solid fellow," added the chief of the Shirogane Station.

"There were two men posing as policemen who called on Mrs. Manabe," said Kawamura.

"Actually, there were probably two men outside your house," said Suzuki-san to Kawamura. "One followed your wife, the other must have broken into your place and conducted the search."

"Any results yet from investigating my house?" asked Kawamura staring at his hands.

"The same marks on the lock that we noticed at Manabe's apartment," answered Suzuki-san.

"Professional," observed Chief Arai, staring at

Disney employees in duck costumes skipping past the picnic table.

"And," added Suzuki-san, "we're pretty certain your son smokes. I said we found cigarette ashes on the floor, but we found a pack of cigarettes under his mattress."

"Professionals wouldn't smoke during a search," said Chief Arai, still looking at the dancing ducks.

"I thought of that," said Kawamura. "We'd have smelled the smoke."

The policemen at the table stared into space. Chief Arai looked as if he was about to jump up and strangle one of the ducks.

"Can I ask a question, Chief Arai?" asked Kawamura after a moment.

Chief Arai rubbed his large hand slowly over his face.

"Yes?"

"What's the status . . . with you? Are you off-duty, or what?"

The other policemen all managed to look in different directions.

"It's a fair question, Kawamura-kun," replied Chief Arai. "I've been relieved of my responsibilities at the Azabu Police Station, and I'm awaiting reassignment. Could be back to Hokkaido."

"Because of this?"

Chief Arai didn't answer for a moment. Instead, he picked up a napkin holder on the picnic table and threw it at the lead duck. The ducks, bills grinning inanely, rapidly waddled away.

"Because of this," confirmed Chief Arai. "They

don't think I completely stopped the investigation."

"I'm sorry," said Kawamura. "It's my fault, but you *did* officially stop the investigation. I . . . ," Kawamura paused. There was nothing else to say.

"I think I know who's responsible at headquarters," said the Chief of the Shirogane Station. He and Chief Arai were contemporaries.

"Who?" asked Kawamura, suddenly regretting the question.

"None of your business," answered Chief Arai.

The policemen at the table stared in different directions.

"Look," said Chief Arai at last. *"They* have their network . . . "

"Who's 'they'?" asked the policeman from Chiba.

"The people we're talking about, you idiot," replied Chief Arai.

"He doesn't know about . . . ," interjected Kawamura.

"OK, I'm sorry," said Chief Arai. "The Kempeitai have their network. The two men in blue suits, or however the hell many there were, were probably part of the old-boy network. But *we* have *ours.*"

The chief from Shirogane nodded.

"My boss doesn't know anything about this," said the man from Ueno. "He just told me to take . . . a vacation. But I don't like it."

"He knows," said Chief Arai. "And you stay out of it. If we need him, *I'll* contact him."

"What do we do?" asked Kawamura after a moment.

"Nothing for the time being," answered Chief Arai. "We'll see who we can link to your friend Ambassador Morimoto. But unless we can prove who killed Shig Manabe in the first place, there's not much we can do. There is no hard evidence for anything after that."

The policemen stared into space. They were eventually interrupted by two Disney security guards in pale blue uniforms followed by a grinning duck.

"Is there a problem here?" asked the first security officer. He had sideburns and pimples.

"Yes," said Chief Arai, formerly of the Azabu Police Station, now rising with the other policemen at the picnic table. "We were assaulted by this goose standing next to you, and we'd like to make a formal complaint to your management."

CHAPTER 43

Suzuki-san drove Captain Kawamura back to the hospital in Chiba and sat with him in the waiting room on the ragged couch for an hour. Kawamura's wife had undergone surgery on her skull to relieve pressure on the brain, but results would not be conclusive for another four or five hours.

The bleeding in Kawamura's daughter had been isolated to a ruptured artery in her stomach, and surgery at about the time of the duck fiasco at Disneyland had effectively solved that problem. She was being fed intravenously, but she was still not conscious.

Kawamura's son was awake and in a traction device seemingly designed by a mad physics professor. Kawamura talked to him for several minutes—until the nurse ordered him out of the room—but he did not mention the cigarettes. There was something about a professional search of one's private living area that, although necessary in this case, nevertheless smacked of a privacy invasion beyond normal expectations.

It was Saturday night—one week after the discovery of Shig Manabe's body in the Tokyo Lawn Tennis Club bath—but Kawamura's life had changed by centuries.

"Our people report that no one of a suspicious nature visited the hospital," said Suzuki-san.

"They probably think they've scared me off," said Kawamura, rubbing a beard a day-and-a-half old.

"Have they?"

"What do you think?"

Suzuki-san rubbed his hand over a head-stubble that was two days old.

"I'd think," said Suzuki-san, "that Chief Arai's networking will take six months or more."

"At the minimum," said Kawamura. "And what do we do in the meantime? Live in fear of someone coming after us for the memoirs?"

"That's not an attractive thought," answered

Suzuki-san. "I remember my grandmother telling me that water brought to a boil rapidly is as hot as water simmering to a boil."

"Was your grandmother a cop?"

"No," answered Suzuki-san, "she ran a soba shop."

"Can you drive me home?" asked Kawamura.

"Of course," replied Suzuki-san. "But only if you tell me what your plan is."

"When I figure out what my plan is," said Kawamura, "you'll be the first to know. Do you think the family is safe here?"

"They'll be safe here," said Suzuki-san rising. "Some of the Chiba people are watching them. Unofficially, of course."

CHAPTER 44

Suzuki-san came into Kawamura's house and the two men sat around for an hour or so discussing the situation. They also ate everything in the house that could be heated in the toaster-oven.

"The best solution would be to convince Mrs. Manabe to publish the memoirs right away," suggested Suzuki-san.

"Chief Arai was right about one thing. That would just take the pressure off us. It still wouldn't prove that Shig Manabe . . . or anyone else was

deliberately murdered by Morimoto and his associates. Besides," added Kawamura, "from what I
understand, publishers screw around forever getting manuscripts converted into books."

"Do you want me to take that?" asked Suzuki-
san looking at the briefcase containing the memoirs.

"The disk is still . . . ?"

"In the mail," confirmed Suzuki-san.

"I may as well keep it here," said Kawamura
after a moment. "If anyone comes for it, they can
have it."

Suzuki-san rose to leave, picking up a banana
in the process and putting it in his pocket.

"I'll be back tomorrow morning to pick you up."

"What for?"

"Take you back out to the hospital."

"No," said Kawamura. "Tomorrow's Sunday.
Take the day off and spend it with your . . . wife.
And that's an order."

Suzuki-san reluctantly agreed, but with the
proviso that Kawamura be careful at all times,
and particularly not continue any aspect of the
investigation without him.

After Suzuki-san left, Kawamura walked through
the rooms. The experts from the station had
probably gone into every nook and cranny in the
place. His son's room looked moderately neater
than it had been, but Kawamura could sense that
things were not in their right place. His son never
put his schoolbooks on the pillow, or his baseball
glove on the floor.

Kawamura walked into his daughter's room and sat on her bed. If anything, the room was neater than it had ever been. Kawamura laid his head back on his daughter's pillow. He recognized her scent. On the ceiling—Kawamura had not noticed this before—were pictures of Disney characters and an American pop-music star. The pop-music star was pretty, but Kawamura had no idea whether it was a man or a woman.

Kawamura closed his eyes. The scent of his daughter—now unconscious in a hospital bed—was even stronger. As tears began to form in the corners of his eyes, he vowed to begin looking for a job that would never place his family in jeopardy again. He was shocked, upon awakening in the morning, that he had slept for ten straight hours.

The first thing Kawamura did was check the Shig Manabe manuscript. He had placed it on the floor near the front door, with a bell between the pages which would drop and wake him if anyone picked up the documents. Everything was as he left it.

He put the last piece of bread in the house in the toaster-oven, then shaved and showered. He emerged from the shower to discover that the bread had become charcoal. Putting on casual slacks and a sport shirt, Kawamura decided that breakfast at the coffee shop near the train station was preferable anyway.

The subway and train connections from

Kawamura's house to Chiba were not ideal, but he was able to make it to the hospital in an hour. Given the heavy volume of cars on the roads during warm summer weekends—including most likely his neighbor's—public transportation was at least quicker.

Kawamura entered the third-floor waiting room, after having been stopped by a fit-looking young man lounging against the elevator. He was an off-duty policeman from the Chiba Station who just happened to be hanging around the hospital at noon on Sunday.

Kawamura's brother-in-law was seated on the ragged couch with two large cardboard boxes apparently containing television sets on the floor in front of him.

"They can't use them," the brother-in-law slurred. He had been drinking again.

"How are they?" Kawamura asked.

"They're perfect. Built-in tape-deck capacity and . . ."

"I mean . . . never mind," said Kawamura walking down the corridor to his wife's room.

Noriko's sister was in the room, and a nurse was hovering protectively nearby. Noriko was conscious, but groggy. Her head was now completely covered with bandages, and she had a padded steel brace on her neck.

"Hi," said Kawamura, "how do you feel?"

"Headache," answered his wife hoarsely. "The kids?"

"They're fine," Kawamura lied. He had no idea

how the kids were. "They're young, and will bounce back."

Noriko Kawamura smiled slightly as her husband bent down and kissed her.

"I'm not that old," she said.

"You just work on getting yourself better," said Kawamura. He held her hand.

"I'm sorry. I don't know what happened."

"It wasn't your fault," said Kawamura as the nurse moved closer to the bed. The visit was over.

Kawamura and Noriko's sister left the room.

"They say her neck was not broken," said the sister-in-law, "but she suffered compressive trauma, whatever that means. They say it's good that she can feel the pins they put in her toes."

"I'm glad," said Kawamura, not knowing what that meant. "Is there a doctor around we can talk to?"

"He'll be back about eight o'clock tonight."

"I'll talk to him then," said Kawamura.

His sister-in-law went back to the waiting room while Kawamura entered his daughter's room. She looked very pale, but she was awake. She was no longer receiving blood transfusions.

"I slept in your bed last night, honey," said Kawamura smelling his daughter's hair.

"I hope you didn't make a mess in my room," said the child of chaos.

"Believe me, you wouldn't notice. How do you feel?"

"I have broken ribs, Papa, but the bleeding inside me stopped. I have to lie very still."

Kawamura brushed her hair away from her forehead. His daughter looked very weak.

"Tell me," Kawamura said, "who is that . . . person on the ceiling of your room?"

His daughter smiled slightly, then closed her eyes.

"Mickey Mouse," she said after a moment. Kawamura watched her as she fell asleep.

Kawamura's son was in the midst of an argument with an old man with no teeth in the bed next to him. Kawamura's son was contending that the Tokyo Giants—even with the former super star Nagashima as the new manager—play old-fashioned baseball. The Seibu Lions, in his son's opinion, were modern and more exciting. The old man was chuckling, or gurgling, and waving his hand dismissively.

"I saw him, Papa," said Kawamura's son after a moment of discussing his condition. His bandages on his arm and shoulders were colossal.

"Who?"

"The man driving the van. He forced us off the road. On purpose."

"You saw him?"

"He looked at me in the eyes. Then he smiled."

"That bas . . . that jerk. What did he look like?"

"He was even older than you," said Kawamura's son innocently, "and had short, curly hair. I remember because he was dressed up in a business suit and tie. Usually people driving vans wear more normal clothing."

"He smiled?"

"Yes. Was he *trying* to kill us, Papa?"

"Maybe," said Kawamura. He grabbed his son's good hand in a macho grip. "But we Kawamuras are too tough for that."

"Why was he trying to kill us?"

"There are people in this world like that," said Kawamura after a moment. "But don't worry now. We'll talk about them later."

CHAPTER 45

Kawamura walked out of the hospital without more than a glance into the waiting room where his in-laws sat with their television boxes. He hailed a taxi and was in the train station on the way back to Tokyo in fifteen minutes. He went beyond the transfer point to his house and rode all the way to Tokyo Station, located in the center of the city.

From there he took a combination of subways to Hiroo—the closest exit to the Tokyo Lawn Tennis Club. He walked up the hill toward the club. Kawamura had no specific plan, other than perhaps to get a look again at former Ambassador Morimoto. He wanted to see the man who figured so prominently in Shig Manabe's memoirs, and who had associates who grinned at children while trying to kill them.

Kawamura did not go to the front entrance of the club. Instead he approached the rear of the facility, near the area by the practice board where he and Suzuki-san had talked to the court manager and head groundsman. The club, occupying about one-half a city block, was completely enclosed by fencing. The rear portion was enclosed by a cement wall two meters high. It was the middle of the afternoon, and Kawamura could hear the thwack of balls being hit and the occasional outbursts of players shouting in triumph or failure.

At the corner, there was a break in the cement wall. A gate led into the property at a point where a small wooden house squatted behind tennis court netting.

Kawamura walked through the gate and was immediately greeted by a woman hanging towels out to dry on a line strung across a small garden.

"This is a private club," said the woman.

"I know that," said Kawamura. "Who are you?"

"Who are you?" demanded the woman. She exuded a strong sense of proprietorship.

Kawamura showed the woman his police identification. He hoped she was not part of the Kempeitai network.

The woman studied the identification carefully.

"The entrance to the club is on the other side," said the woman finally. She pointed back out to the sidewalk.

"I understand that too," said Kawamura gently. "But now that you know me, who are you?"

"My husband and I live here. We have worked at the club for over forty years. My name," stated the woman proudly, "is Naba."

"I think I know your husband," said Kawamura pleasantly. "I think he is the head groundsman?"

"Of course. Without him, there wouldn't *be* a club."

"I agree with you completely. I'll wait right here, but would you tell him that the 'baseball policeman' is back? I want to talk to him about the club . . . privately."

Mrs. Naba looked at Kawamura, who smiled back innocently.

"OK," she said. "But wait here."

Naba-san showed up in a surprisingly short time. He was carrying a long-handled brush used to spread clay around the courts and clean up after matches.

"Ah," said Naba-san, "another bet?"

"Maybe later. In the meantime, do you know if the club president is here today?"

"He's always here on weekends. You can walk through here and up to the clubhouse."

"Wait a minute," said Kawamura. "I'll meet him later. I'd just like to watch . . . you know, the tennis games . . . from here. Is there a way . . . ?"

"The way is from my house," said the head groundsman. "I assume your interest in the games is confidential?"

"Yes, it is," answered Kawamura. Naba-san had risen a notch in his estimation of the man.

"Does this have anything to do with the death of Sakai-san?"

Kawamura noted that the issue in Naba's mind was not one involving everyone's friend Shig Manabe, it involved no one's friend Takashi Sakai. No one's friend, that is, except the club employees.

"Yes sir," said Kawamura, "it does."

"The best view is from here," said Naba leading Kawamura into the decidedly humble living quarters. "You can see the clubhouse and all the courts except one."

Naba and his long-handled brush left immediately. Kawamura pulled what appeared to be a bar stool to one of the small windows and sat down. Although accustomed to compact houses, space in this abode was especially cramped. It was obviously a remnant of the original clubhouse structure which had been located at this end of the property.

Straight ahead, five tennis courts away, was the modern clubhouse. The wall of the building facing the courts was made entirely of glass. Kawamura could see members inside sitting at tables or relaxing in chairs. A great deal of activity occurred at or near the area where refreshments were served. The second floor, behind smaller frosted windows, housed the locker rooms and the site of Manabe's last bath.

To his left, across a small corridor running the length of the property, were the other half of the tennis courts. Kawamura could indeed see four of the five courts.

Kawamura sat for ten minutes before he located Morimoto. The president of the club emerged from the clubhouse with three men approximately his age. Walking along the narrow corridor, Morimoto passed other members coming or going to their games. He spoke to each of them, obviously bantering good-naturedly. It was almost as if he were running for public office.

Morimoto and his colleagues played at court number four, one court away from where Kawamura was sitting. Still without a plan, Kawamura nevertheless concentrated on every movement made by Morimoto during the two sets of tennis.

The club president, in Kawamura's unprofessional opinion, played an elegant but not very good game of tennis. He swung his racket with great flourish and an almost schooled follow-through, and he seemed to leap and bound after balls hit in his direction, but the end effect was not always positive. The three men playing with him moved less, seemed to know where the ball was going before it was hit, and swung their rackets with a minimum of movement and effort. It occurred to Kawamura, a man who had never hit a tennis ball with a racket in his life, that Morimoto had learned the game late in life. The other players, in their relaxed way, were carrying the tennis club president.

At the conclusion of two sets, both of which the

president and his partner lost, the four men stood for a moment at the small table next to the net packing their gear and wiping themselves with small towels. Kawamura leaned forward on his stool, but he was too far away to see if Morimoto had a pink scar on the back of his neck.

Morimoto and his colleagues made their way along the narrow corridor back to clubhouse. As before, the club president had something to say to everyone he passed. Kawamura watched them enter the clubhouse, and eventually a waitress delivered beers to the foursome. Kawamura still had no plan, other than the vague urge to isolate Morimoto and bring things to a head by a direct confrontation of some kind.

Kawamura stood up, did two or three deep knee-bends, and stretched his back. He looked at his watch and was surprised to learn that he had been sitting on the bar stool for almost two hours. Although now late afternoon, the heat, particularly in the groundsman's small house, was still stifling.

Morimoto and his friends were still sitting in the clubhouse drinking beer. Kawamura sat on the stool again and watched other players. The Frenchman, Mr. "Too Long" in Kawamura's mind, played an exuberant game—chasing every ball even remotely in his neighborhood—and seemed to succeed at least half the time. Kawamura wondered how the man had any energy left to *cherchez les femmes* after his strenuous heroics.

Theodore Bitman played on the court immediately in front of Kawamura. He was a surprisingly good player. A left-hander, he seemed to over-power—or at least intimidate—his opponents by a combination of skill and bad temper. He'd get mad at himself for mistakes he made, and the tension created as a result would cause his opponents to be wary of shots they'd hit to him. Bitman would jump all over those shots.

Nat Forrest, playing on a court to Kawamura's left, was to tennis what a 40-handicapper is to golf. Kawamura wondered what his fiancée, the waitress, thought of that. Perhaps he had other skills.

Kawamura noticed that Hanada—Shig Manabe's distant relative—and Kimura—Shig Manabe's first employee (and the Miyabe of the memoirs)—played as partners against two foreigners. A combination of drop shots, fluffy returns of serve, and twisting backhands completely annihilated the foreigners who were into power at all times.

Kawamura even recognized the president of the Tokyo American Club, a participant in the drama surrounding a murder investigation two years before, playing on court number three. J. B. Culhane played an adequate game, but refused to chase anything hit beyond a meter from his position. This most probably caused his partner— a prematurely graying Japanese man—to prema-turely develop the gray hair. Could it be, Kawamura asked himself, that tensions and passions on the court could have actually motivated Sakai to clobber his partner Manabe in the bath?

Kawamura looked at the clubhouse again. President Morimoto was gone. Kawamura jumped off the stool and headed for the door of the head groundsman's house.

"Are you going now?" asked Naba as Kawamura emerged into the tiny garden next to the house.

"I, er, thought I'd go and . . . see if I can meet the club president," said Kawamura.

"Take your time," said Naba leaning his long-handled brush against the cement wall. "They are having a special board meeting tonight. It'll take another hour or so."

As Naba said this, a now fully dressed Morimoto joined another seven or eight fully dressed men and women entering a room at the rear of the tennis lounge area.

"They are discussing replacing the clay with an all-weather surface," continued Naba.

"Won't that put you out of work?"

"I hope so," answered Naba. "But they've been discussing the subject for at least fifteen years."

"Is there a way out of the conference room other than the door we can see?"

"No, in fact by the time they're finished, the front entrance of the club will be closed. Everyone will have to leave through the glass doors and go around the side of the clubhouse to the front."

Kawamura and Naba watched the clubhouse in silence for a moment. Finally, Kawamura asked if he could use Naba's phone. Kawamura was led back into the cramped house.

He finally got through to the nurses' station on

the third floor of the hospital and learned that there had been no significant change in anyone's health. His daughter, however, appeared to be coming down with a cold. Coughing and an occasional sneeze were not only very painful with the broken rib condition, some internal bleeding had begun again. The doctor, who would be there in about an hour, might order another blood transfusion, Kawamura was told.

The nurse found Kawamura's sister-in-law and put her on the phone. The sister-in-law was particularly interested in Noriko's condition.

"They still don't know if she'll ever walk again," said the sister-in-law. She was close to tears.

"All we can do is wait," said Kawamura. "The nurse said there is still too much swelling around her neck to be certain of anything yet."

"Will you be here when the doctor arrives to examine her? They say he'll be here at eight."

Kawamura looked at his watch. It was already six-thirty.

He *could* make it back to the hospital in Chiba by eight o'clock if he left the club immediately. But Kawamura had an overwhelming desire to confront Morimoto *now*. Kawamura knew that he'd have to report to work at the police station tomorrow. There'd apparently be a new acting chief in place, Kawamura would be given other assignments, and the Shig Manabe affair—and the related events—would dissolve into an ugly memory too remote to reexamine or investigate.

"I'm sorry, I can't make it back to the hospital by eight. I still have some unfinished business to take care of first."

As Kawamura hung up, he knew that his sister-in-law would never understand, and their relationship, shaky at best, was probably close to being destroyed.

Kawamura turned from the phone and was surprised to see Naba standing in the doorway. He looked at Kawamura with a level gaze, and it was obvious he had been listening to Kawamura's end of the phone conversation. After all, realized Kawamura, it *was* his house and phone.

"Can I help?" asked the head groundsman. Kawamura looked at the man who had readily accepted the double-or-nothing bet.

"Yes," said Kawamura after a moment. "I would like to meet President Morimoto alone."

"*Completely* alone?"

"Completely alone," confirmed Kawamura.

"OK," said Naba, the head groundsman for over forty years.

CHAPTER 46

The sun had set an hour ago. Lights from the clubhouse spilled out and partially illuminated court number one, but the rest of the grounds were dark.

Lights in the business office had been turned off long ago, and the office staff had apparently left the building before the front entrance was locked.

Kawamura noticed Naba once in the clubhouse talking to a waitress, but Naba spent the majority of the time on the courts rolling up the nets in the dark. He had earlier told his wife to go down to a Chinese restaurant in the Juban, explaining that he would join her later.

Kawamura stood in the shadows halfway up the narrow corridor between the two rows of courts. The last of the members had finished their drinks and snacks, and were now laughing their way out of the glass clubhouse doors and around the side of the building to what must have been a small gap between the building and the perimeter fencing.

Within a minute or two, the conference room door at the rear of the lounge area opened and the fully dressed board members began to file out. A couple of members approached the counter and appeared to call out for service, but the waitresses had all gone.

People began to walk out the glass doors and turn to the side exit. Morimoto looked as if he would not only join them but would be in the midst of them. There didn't seem to be a way to isolate him.

Suddenly, Naba appeared from behind the service counter and said something to Morimoto. Morimoto hesitated, then seemed to wave Naba away with a gesture indicating that the subject wasn't important. Morimoto tried to catch up with the last of the board members leaving the clubhouse.

Naba did not give up. He kept talking, and seemed to impart a sense of urgency. Finally, Morimoto shrugged his shoulders, waved good night to the last of the departing board members, and followed Naba through the glass doors. Kawamura heard Naba say, "The problem is with the pole for the nets on the second court," as the two men walked across the first court. It was a subject, Kawamura thought, Morimoto had never even considered before.

Kawamura stepped from the narrow corridor onto court number two. Naba spotted Kawamura's movement and suddenly disappeared into the darkness. Morimoto continued walking and staring toward the shadowy form of a net wrapped around a support pole.

"Lungchi," said Kawamura softly into the warm summer night. It was a place far removed from the 1990s and the wealthy Tokyo neighborhood. It was the prison camp in 1945 in China.

Morimoto froze. He looked in Kawamura's direction.

"I know about it, and I know about you," continued Kawamura walking out of the shadows.

Morimoto stared at Kawamura in silence. He did not move a muscle.

"Shig Manabe's memoirs will soon be part of the public record. And there's nothing you can do about it."

"Who are you?" asked Morimoto, squinting in the darkness. "Ah, you," he said as Kawamura approached. "The policeman."

"You've managed to hide your past until now, but soon the world will know."

"You're talking nonsense, Mr. Policeman. Go back to your traffic tickets."

"Manabe-san identified you as a former Kempeitai officer. And not a very nice one," Kawamura added.

Morimoto, still not moving, stared at Kawamura. If Morimoto said that he didn't know what Kawamura was talking about, Kawamura was not certain what the next step should be. Morimoto, even standing perfectly still in the darkness, had a dominating presence.

"You're a fake, Morimoto. A high-profile, world-revered fake."

That did it. The smooth, diplomatic façade crumbled. Morimoto leaned forward—his face so close that Kawamura could feel the man's hot breath.

"You worthless little piece of shit. What do you know about the Kempeitai? The war? Safe in your mama's belly. You have no right to judge about what went on then. No right."

"That's not my . . ."

"We must do what our country asks of us." Morimoto's voice had risen from a hoarse whisper to a clear snarl. "That is our ultimate responsibility. It was people like Manabe, the soft people, who were the cause of Japan's downfall as much as the atomic bomb."

"But you . . . "

Morimoto was not interested in interruptions.

"I have served my country well in *all* capacities. It is not up to you or that weasel Manabe to make judgment. I have earned respect." Morimoto poked a stiff index finger at Kawamura's shoulder. "You owe your job . . . even your life . . . to people like me. And don't forget it, you insignificant turd."

Kawamura also leaned forward—his face centimeters from Morimoto's.

"Look, Mr. Former Ambassador, I don't know anything about wars that make people behave like animals during those wars. What I *do* know about is the murder of innocent people to save reputations. And the attempted murder," Kawamura realized he was screaming, "of innocent women and children."

Morimoto glared at Kawamura for a moment, then his lips—not his eyes—grinned. His eyes had flickered briefly over Kawamura's left shoulder.

"You'll never prove that, asshole."

Morimoto collected his dignified self and began to turn to leave. Kawamura reached for the man's shoulder. It was then that the blow, unbelievably painful, hit him the area of the kidneys.

CHAPTER 47

Kawamura felt the flesh on his left cheek ripped away by the coarse clay on the tennis court. For some reason he was on the ground, a heavy weight was on his back, and someone was kicking him as he squirmed and kept trying to regain his feet.

He glanced up once and saw Morimoto hurrying toward the side exit to the right of the clubhouse. Between blows to the back of his head, Kawamura saw Morimoto bounce off a dark form that had just entered the exit. Morimoto turned, and ran through the glass doors into the clubhouse.

Kawamura was kicked again in the kidney, and the pain was excruciating. He was afraid he'd pass out. He felt more kicks to a rapidly numbing body.

Suddenly, a massive collision seemed to remove all weight from Kawamura's back. He looked back briefly and saw bodies rolling around on the ground in the darkness.

Kawamura got up and dashed toward the clubhouse and Morimoto. He nearly fell twice—the blows to his back and legs had damaged normal coordination and strength.

Kawamura staggered through the glass doors. Morimoto had already run through the wooden doors to the entrance lobby of the club. The front doors to the club, Kawamura remembered, were locked.

Kawamura opened the wooden doors. The front doors to the club were closed. He looked up, probably because of the faint sound of steps, at the circular stairway leading to the locker rooms. It may have been his imagination, but he thought he caught a glimpse of shoes disappearing at the top of the stairs. If so, Morimoto was trapped. And now hiding.

Kawamura bent over and slipped off his shoes. He then, very carefully, climbed the circular stairway. Passing the elk head, he reached the landing at the entrance to the locker rooms.

Kawamura would have thought that the women's locker room, at this time of night, would be the more logical place to hide. Morimoto, on the other hand, was in a panic. And panic did not result in logic.

Kawamura turned left and very slowly entered the men's locker room. He made it through the entranceway where tennis rackets were stored and almost as far as the toilets where the cigarette butt was discovered.

The blow to the side of his head made his brain explode with a blinding light. Glass seemed to be breaking in his skull. Kawamura reeled back against a locker, opened his eyes, and saw that Morimoto was swinging again at him with a tennis racket. It was a looping overhead shot—a shot Kawamura realized would have an exaggerated follow-through.

Kawamura ducked to his left as the edge of Morimoto's racket smashed into the side of a locker. Kawamura picked up a racket from the storage area in time to fend off a wildly swinging forehand to his midsection. The men were dueling as samurai of yore—but with tennis rackets.

Morimoto wound up for another looping swing at Kawamura's head. Kawamura remembered watching him on the tennis court. Kawamura jabbed his racket straight ahead and smashed it into Morimoto's throat. Morimoto reeled backwards into the bath area. Kawamura followed up with what he later learned was a backhand shot to Morimoto's right elbow.

Morimoto, still reeling backwards, switched hands and swung at Kawamura with his left hand. Kawamura hit Morimoto diagonally across the chest.

Morimoto was off-balance. His legs were crossed as the result of flailing away at random. He took one more twisting step to the rear. The floor was slippery.

Kawamura hit him with the first overhead shot he had ever attempted in his life. Morimoto's lead foot slipped out from under him. He fell backwards—his head crashing onto the rim of the club bath.

Kawamura was still bent over catching his breath when Suzuki-san reached the locker room.

"Dead?" asked Suzuki-san simply.

"I think so," said Kawamura. "He attacked me."

Both men looked at the former Ambassador to the United States and current President of the Tokyo Lawn Tennis Club lying on the floor next to the bath. Kawamura reached forward and turned Morimoto's head to the side. A pink scar was clearly visible on the back of his neck. His blood was beginning to mix with the water on the floor next to the bath.

Kawamura and his assistant Suzuki-san walked in silence down the circular stairway. They walked through the well-lit but empty clubhouse to the tennis courts. Handcuffed to the net-pole of court number one were two men—one unconscious and flat on his back. The other man was vigorously rubbing his short curly hair with his free hand. Both were wearing dark blue suits.

"You promised that you'd tell me if you were going to try anything," accused Suzuki-san.

"I know that," said Kawamura. "This just sort of developed."

Both men stood on the steps outside the clubhouse and looked at the two captives.

"How did you know I'd be here?" asked Kawamura.

"If you weren't home, or at the hospital, where would you be?" said Suzuki-san.

Kawamura put his arm around Suzuki-san's blue serge shoulder.

"I appreciate it, my friend."

"A day's work," said Suzuki-san noncommittally.

"What about them?" asked Kawamura, indicating the two men handcuffed to the net-pole.

"Possession of stimulant drugs with an intent to sell," explained Suzuki-san. "A tremendous quantity."

"Really?'

"Well, at least by the time we get back to the station," said Suzuki-san.

The due-process concept in Japan is cloaked in gray.

"What about Morimoto upstairs?" asked Suzuki-san.

"I don't know anything about it," said Kawamura, rubbing his lower back. "In fact, I've decided to take the day off tomorrow. It's somebody else's problem. I'm going back to the hospital. We've already solved the murder at the Tokyo Lawn Tennis Club."

— THE END —

Epilogue

The President of the Tokyo Lawn Tennis Club and former Ambassador to the United States Tatsuo Morimoto was grieved far and wide by those sensitive to the importance of a subtle understanding of international relations. His accidental death in the clubhouse of the tennis club was merely another example of the frailty of life and the universality of sudden death striking the great and small. His funeral was well attended, and many nice things were said about the man.

With considerably less fanfare, two retired individuals named Sasaki and Imamura were convicted and sentenced to twenty years in prison for their crime of introducing the evil of narcotic drugs to the innocent youth of Japan. Appeals for clemency were not heard by the presiding judge.

Chief Arai, retrieved from a fishing trip in his native Hokkaido, was reinstated as head of the Azabu Police Station. He immediately fell into the routine of yelling at Kawamura during the morning staff meetings.

Nat Forrest's engagement to a waitress at the Tokyo Lawn Tennis Club was broken due to expanding and irreconcilable interests.

Shirley Manabe, a woman who had been married to one of the nicest guys on earth, decided that Shig's memoirs should *not* be published until the manuscript had been edited—a process she reckoned would take at least five years.

Kawamura's son was the first to completely recover from his injuries in the automobile accident. He returned home to find a new computer capable, with adaptors, of accepting any disk known to man.

Kawamura's daughter also recovered, but the road was longer and more difficult. An abscess had developed where one of the broken ribs had punctured her lung, and she spent three months in the hospital receiving intravenous doses of antibiotics.

Noriko Kawamura was the star of the show. Despite a lingering but gradually receding tingling in her extremities—a feeling that her feet and hands had gone to sleep—her head and neck injuries responded to the prescribed therapy.

Kawamura has still not found a job equaling the money and challenge of his current occupation—the old "burst-bubble" problem—but he's still looking. Despite the daily arguments with Chief Arai, no one including Arai questioned Kawamura's request for a leave of absence during the New Year season.

Kawamura finally took the family to Disneyland, but the venture was in the Big Time. The trip to Southern California and the *real* Disneyland was an unforgettable experience for the family. Stopping in Hawaii on the way home was also fun, but a small event had a sudden and sobering impact on Kawamura. At the Pearl Harbor Memorial, Kawamura found himself praying for *all* the war dead of *all* nations. This, he realized, included Suzuki the yakitori man, and the Silver Fox team.

Suzuki-san and his "wife" met the Kawamura family at Narita Airport when they returned from the United States. The only jarring note in the reunion was that Suzuki-san's woman-of-the-moment, smiling, looking very attentive, was the waitress from the Tokyo Lawn Tennis Club.